Also by Joe Corso

The Comeback
The Time Portal
Lafitte's Treasure
Gunfight in Abilene
Shootout in Cheyenne
The Last Gun-Shark
the Lone Jack Kid series
The Revenge of John W
The Time Traveler series
The Starlight Club series
The Old Man and the King
Engine 24 Fire Stories series
Tommy Topper and the Pixie Princess

www.corsobooks.com

The Old Man
and the King

Joe Corso

Black Horse Publishing
www.blackhorsepublishing.com

First printing

To all the Korean Veterans—the forgotten warriors.

TABLE OF CONTENTS

Prologue

The men left the Dakota Hotel on the Upper West Side of Manhattan fifteen minutes earlier than they had planned. They hoped it would give them the edge they needed to get safely to their destination. Driving against the snowstorm felt like being marooned on a celestial snowbound planet, driving to some place that didn't exist. Sheets of snow obstructed their view of the black Mercedes, following them a half city block behind. The driver struggled to navigate the large military Hummer. Its wheels couldn't seem to find traction on the blizzard-covered roads. The men in the Hummer were experts, but the snow was robbing them of their professionalism, causing them to focus more on keeping the car on the road rather than on what was going on behind them. Stranded and abandoned vehicles lined the Manhattan streets.

Seventy-Second Street East seemed safer. It was a wider street. The men took it to Second Avenue, down to Forty-Second Street. Visibility was becoming more difficult. Slowly, the car pulled alongside the curb and stopped. The driver turned to the man sitting between two large men in the back seat. "Your Majesty, it's not safe to drive any farther. We'll have to walk the rest of the way."

"Where are we now?" the passenger asked.

"We're on Forty-Second Street. The U.N. is only one block east of here."

The King turned to his Secretary of State. "Claude, did you call U.N. Security to let them know we will need a conference room to use while we wait our turn before the council?"

"Yes, Your Majesty. It's I have arranged all. They have a conference room waiting for you. You can relax there until you're called to speak."

"What if the U.N. decides not to hold hearings today because of the weather? Do we have that covered?"

"Yes, Your Majesty, because either way, once we're inside the U.N., we'll be safe under the protection of the U.N. Security team."

"Well, let's not keep the U.N. waiting. Let's go."

The front door of the Hummer opened and a large military-looking man stepped out from the passenger seat. He sported a crew cut, had a bold, prominent forehead, and eyes as big as an eagle's. He looked up and down the block through waves of heavily falling snow, carefully analyzing any suspicious-looking movements. Satisfied, he nodded to the others, signaling that it was safe to exit the car. The Secretary of State was the first one out, followed by the King's security detail. As protocol dictated, the King was always last. The King inched his way closer to the open door. As the important man was about to emerge, a hail of gunfire erupted from the south side of the street.

The King watched in shock as, one by one, the car's occupants fell limply to the ground. For a moment, he remained rooted to his seat, trying to grasp the gravity of the situation. First, they had leveled his Secretary of State with a bullet, then the others, right before his eyes. The gunfire was coming from the passenger side. Through the window, the King could see the assassins and their car, a black Mercedes.

The King slid to the opposite side, opened the door, and placed his body low into the snow. He crawled quickly, trying to avoid the slaughter that was taking place on the other side of the car. First, it was two feet, then six, then ten, until he deemed it a safe enough distance to run. He wore a Russian ushanka - the fur hat with earflaps that Russians wear to keep their head and ears warm during the cold Russian winters. He tugged on the flaps, pulled up his collar, and trotted through the blinding snow, holding onto the hope that he could make it across the avenue into the safety of the U.N. building.

Back at the King's car, the snow wove a cloak of white, covering the blood-soaked bodies of the dead men. A host of armed strangers surrounded the bodies.

"Find the King," a deep voice ordered.

Methodically, the men began flipping over each dead body, searching for the one man most important to all of them. They dressed one particular body the way a king might be. They smelled victory. The leader of the assassins removed a photo from his inside coat pocket and examined each face carefully. He held the photo in his icy gloved hands and stared at it, but no matter how hard he wished, he had to reconcile the fact that the dead man in front of him was not the King. This did not please him. The blizzard was worsening, and the men were freezing.

Annoyed, the man said, "I know he was here with the others. He had to be. He was addressing the U.N. today."

The leader looked in all four directions as if willing the snow to stop. It was a blizzard like nothing he had ever experienced, even in his homeland, and he sure as hell didn't want to be outside any longer than he had to be.

"Damnit! With all the gunfire and confusion, he must have slipped out of the car and run off, but where could he have gone?" he huffed.

"He must have headed toward the U.N. That's the only place that would be safe for him," another man chimed in.

The leader nodded his head. "Good thinking, Jimmy. Get in the car. That's where we're heading."

There was irony in this weather, leading to a curious twist of fate. The men's sole purpose tonight was to kill the King in conditions that would be inconspicuous and now, he, the King, was invisible, all because of a blanket of snow—the very conditions that should have worked against him.

The King was all alone, in a foreign city, in less than ideal weather. He quickly surmised that calling home was probably not a good idea. Surely, the murmurs weren't true. He had been told by a top advisor that his brother was jealous of him and his power and had showed that they had overheard a conversation. While details were unknown, the conversation seemed to be unfavorable toward the King. The King did not know whom to trust.

Now, with the U.N. clearly in sight, all the King had to do was walk across the street and alert security that he had arrived. At his precise moment of hope, a black Mercedes fishtailed around the corner. He ducked into an alleyway next to a closed deli and hid behind a dumpster. The smell was horrific, but not nearly as horrendous as the smell of death, he thought. He waited anxiously, wondering if his pursuers knew of his whereabouts. Crouching next to a wall, he glimpsed up the street and watched as the car disappeared into the storm.

Chapter One

The old man looked at his alarm clock. It was four a.m. Darn, he was cold. "Must be something wrong with the heat 'cuz I'm freezing," he said out loud to himself. Shivering, he climbed out of bed and headed toward the thermostat. Thinking it might be stuck, he banged on it. From the corner of his eye, he caught a glance of something moving. It surprised him to see snow falling already–They didn't expect it until much later in the day. The meteorologist was wrong again. It was a heck of a time for his heat to stop working.

The old man flipped on the shower, and it surprised him to find that he had hot water. Hot water, but no heat. Curious. He stepped into the tiny cubicle and let the warm water soothe his muscles, hoping to neutralize the chill from the room. He stepped out from the shower and wasted no time dressing quickly without shaving. Just as quickly, he bundled himself in an undershirt, coat, and scarf. He pulled his scarf taut around his neck, covered his ears with an old woolen cap, and donned his gloves before opening the door to brave the cold.

The old man was seventy-two years old and trim, with a surprising amount of musculature. He had a thick head of gray hair. Originally from the hills of Tennessee, he had settled in New York City after being discharged from the service. His friend Charlie lived here. There was a time when he was five feet eleven, but that was when he was in the army. He seemed to have shrunk a little because when he visited the VA to get his prescriptions renewed; they measured him at five nine. How the hell did I lose two inches? He thought. Every morning and every evening, he still did fifty pushups, just like he had done every day since he was twelve years old. While in the army, even after a rough day in the field, he continued this discipline before turning in each night. He would continue to do so unless rendered incapable or until he died. By doing pushups, he was letting his body know that he wasn't quite through yet, but truth be told, Lom liked to exercise, only now with old age, it was becoming a bit of a chore. Still, guilt set in if he missed a day. He thought of cutting back to thirty or forty a day, but he knew that if he did, he might soon do twenty and then what... ten? No, he knew he had to push himself to do the fifty. There were some other changes in his body. He was stooping a lot lately and had become self-conscious that he was walking like little old men do. Whenever he caught himself standing hunchbacked, he would immediately straighten up and curse himself for letting it happen yet again.

The yin and the yang. But at this moment, the city looked like a wintry Christmas card, beautiful and unspoiled. It was really a privilege to see what many New Yorkers wouldn't. At this hour, most were still hugging their pillows. If only they could see their city as it looked now, they might recognize its grandeur, so often taken for granted. Probably not, he second-guessed–too close to the trees to see the forest. The city that never sleeps, oddly enough, did at this time of the morning. At least it did if there were far fewer taxis, and except for the occasional drunk stumbling out of an all-night bar, it remained quiet and still.

The icy cold bit deep into the old man's bones, right through to his toes. The combat boots and thick woolen socks, purchased from the same army/navy surplus store where he bought his woolen army cap, did little to stave off the numbness that was settling in. Exhaled breaths formed puffs of smoke and while he had stopped smoking around twenty years ago, it reminded him of the dirty little habit that he sometimes missed, much like an old lover's embrace, but common sense always prevailed. The only benefit from smoking was to the cigarette companies.

It was still dark when he arrived at the Good Burger, a small eatery in midtown Manhattan on Second Avenue, but now there were signs of life. It was a little breakfast oasis nestled in the concrete of the Big Apple. Only four-thirty a.m. and he could smell the morning's preparations. As he opened the door to the eatery, a blast of cold air followed him into the store right to his seat. He sat for a moment, not quite content that he'd warmed up yet.

"Hi, Martha," he said.

"Hi, Lom. You're up early this morning. Couldn't sleep? Or did your girlfriend leave you for another man?"

The old man smiled. He liked Martha, and they had become friends over the years, always bantering back and forth and making one another smile over a silly remark here and there. That was why he kept coming back here, to see Martha, to be among familiar faces.

"You got that right, Martha. It was just too damned cold in my place this morning. I'm planning on asking Charlie to look at what happened to the heat. He's good at fixing those kinds of things, and I know he'll jump right on it when I tell him about it."

Martha was a redhead, about fifty years of age, and a tad on the portly side. She was an attractive woman. Lom thought she must have been a real looker in her youth. Martha had been working nine to six-night shift for about seven years, maybe longer, but Lom could only count the seven years that he'd been coming here.

"What'll you have for breakfast, Lom?"

"I think I'll have bacon and eggs over easy with whole wheat toast," he said as he finally braved relieving himself of the coat. "And a nice cup of steaming hot black coffee. That should warm my innards up a bit."

"Double over easy, whole wheat," she yelled to the short-order cook. "Meanwhile, here's your coffee," she said as she leaned over the table. "Here ya go. Hot coffee to warm you, my friend. It's fresh. Just made it a few minutes ago."

"Thanks, Martha," he said, placing his hands around the hot cup, hoping to warm his fingers a bit.

Chapter Two

Lom spotted them as they got out of the black Mercedes that had slid to a stop, parking at an angle in front of the eatery. There were four of them. One stayed in the car behind the wheel. The other three stood in a circle, casually sneaking looks into the eatery through the large plate-glass window. Apparently, they were expecting to meet someone here, but why didn't they just come in? They were all dressed in the same–black leather overcoats and black Russian style fur hats. Lom sensed something odd. From his booth in the diner, he studied the men. They kept looking to either side, checking out the streets. Each man took turns cupping his hands against the diner glass, looking at the patrons with interest. A crescendo of chatter and bold hand gestures ensued. Something clearly frustrated the men at something. Sensing defeat, Lom watched as the men returned to the car and hastily made a retreat, causing the car to fishtail and slide in the slick ice that lay underneath the snow, their rear wheels swerving to gain traction. The driver somehow maneuvered the car back onto the street and off they sped. Oh well, Lom thought. Weird. Sometimes this city was just plain odd. It attracted all kinds. He took another sip of coffee.

From the recessed entrance of a nearby store, a young man peered out of the shadows. He looked carefully in both directions before stepping onto the sidewalk. Satisfied that all was safe, he brushed himself off and entered the eatery. He'd be safe here at least for a little while, he thought. He seated himself in a booth facing the diner's entrance and ordered nothing more than coffee. The young man was a handsome blond lad about six feet, early twenties, dressed in a suit that, judging by the tailored look and cut, appeared to be a designer. He walked with a gait of masculine refinement, had smart eyes, but appeared frightened and fidgety. Lom felt the impulse to ask if he was all right, but the black Mercedes interrupted the overture. Once again, it glided to a stop right smack in front of the diner. This time, Lom zeroed in on a gun that one of them had holstered to his waist. The others had something cupped in their hands, trying hard to conceal them. Guns. They all had guns.

The streets were almost barren and the few customers in the restaurant were too busy having their early morning wake up meal to notice anything unusual. Lom looked around and counted the occupied seats–four men seated at the counter, three booths had customers, he and the kid, being two of them. Two construction workers sat in the other.

The three Mercedes men entered the restaurant. One man stationed himself by the door. Suddenly, a man brandishing a gun yelled, "Everyone in the back! Now! Not you," he said, pointing to the kid. "You stay seated. Don't move!" he said in a slight accent. "You, old man, get in back with the others."

"Can I at least finish my eggs and coffee?" the old man replied, as though nothing was odd about men in black leather and ushankas waving weapons. "I can't afford to waste my money on a second helping," Lom continued.

"Are you crazy?" another one snapped, speaking perfect English. He had no accent at all. "You get back there or I'll a put a bullet right through you. Which do you want–eggs and coffee, or a bullet?"

"Well, when you explain it like that, I guess I'll join the others," he said calmly.

The old man found himself at the front of the group, facing three men in black with accents, holding guns. His mind was racing. The one at the door wouldn't be a problem, he thought. Neither would the leader, but the one pointing the gun at the kid was a big problem. The third man walked over to where the kid was. He pulled out his gun and said something in a foreign language. The kid glared back at him and said something back. Instinctively, the patrons dropped to the floor, covering their heads, never looking up. With that, the man raised his gun and steadily held it about ten inches from the kid's head. He cocked the gun, taking aim at his forehead. The patrons, hearing this, let out screams almost in unison. Then, at lightning speed, pop, pop, boom–three firecracker-sounding explosions rang out from nowhere. One bullet plowed into the center of the gunman's chest, propelling him across four booths and crashing him into a fifth, where he tumbled to the floor. Another bullet slammed bull's eye into the heart of the man by the door. It hit the third man just above his right eye; the momentum taking part in his skull with it. The old man never removed the gun from his clothes. He quickly took his hands out of his pocket and dropped to the floor, feigning fear and shock, like all the others, his right side pocket facing the floor. He reached his right hand down over the outside of the pocket to cover the three perfectly carved holes. As if in slow motion, one by one, the customers rose, looking at each other questioningly, but still too afraid to speak. One of the construction workers broke the silence.

"Is everybody okay? Is anybody hit?" the construction worker asked. The patrons and staff were busy turning over their hands, checking their clothes, searching for clues that perhaps they'd been injured in the madness. Each person nodded that he or she was clear of any injuries. "The gunshots here were loud," he stammered. "There was nobody else in the room but us, not unless someone shot from across the street, but the gunshots were loud, like they were right here."

Martha calmly reached for the phone and called the police. The storm would hinder their arrival, she was told, but weather permitting, they'd have a car there in a few minutes.

Slowly, each of the patrons took turns talking, trying to assess who, what, where. It was the "who" that had them all stumped. Oddly, no one saw who fired the three deadly shots. They were all too busy ducking for cover, too fearful to look up at the travesty that was about to occur. The old man walked over to the kid, careful to keep his right hand over the three holes carved into his pocket. Grabbing him by the arm, he pulled him aside and said, "Come on. You'd better come with me."

With the doors to the restaurant closed and the howling noise of the wind, the Mercedes driver hadn't heard the commotion inside. There was a light tap on his window that startled him a bit. The driver looked up to see an old man motioning for him to roll down his window. He waved him away, but the old man persisted. The driver pressed the button and had opened the window just halfway when the piercing metal landed in his temple, splattering blood and brain matter throughout the impeccably clean interior of the car. The old man calmly reached inside the car, removed the cell phone resting on the dash, and placed it in his pocket. With his arm hooked around the kid's, he stepped over the curb and onto the sidewalk, careful not to slip on the ice.

"Looks like some mighty bad people are looking for you, young fella. You'll be safe where I'm taking you. When we're all warm and settled in, you can tell me all about it over a cup of coffee. Does that sound like a plan, son?" he asked as he raised his right arm and patted the kid on the shoulder. The kid glared at the three holes in his pocket and barely nodded his head, finding it difficult to process what had just happened. This old man had just shot and killed four men, saving a stranger's life, and he was acting like it was just another day's work.

The diner was buzzing with cops, questioning everyone who had been in the place when the shooting occurred — customers and staff. No one had any explanations. The survivors described how they were all herded to the back of the store. They told where the gunmen positioned themselves and the odd way they dressed. Martha told them how one gunman had held a gun to a young man's head, recounting the gunman's words of "sorry," and the rest in some other language, and how he was going to have to kill him. That was it. She, too, had nothing more to offer. After she completed her eyewitness account, she made a hasty retreat to the counter and started brewing a fresh pot of coffee. Martha was holding up well—so well that she found it hard to contain her smile. She had to be careful, lest she give herself away. From where she was standing, she had seen Lom fire his gun right through his heavy winter coat with an accuracy that amazed her. Lom single-handedly had killed all three bad guys and had saved multiple lives by doing so.

Chapter Three

"What do you mean you haven't heard from them? You mean nobody called in?" a deep, stern voice asked.

"No. I've been waiting all morning for an update and nothing," another answered.

"Did you try getting them on their cell phones?" he asked, clearly annoyed.

"All morning, boss."

"And no answer?"

"None. I know nothing. Maybe the snow is affecting the cell signal."

"Nah, the snow shouldn't make a difference. For Christ's sake, the kid was alone. How hard is it to find the kid? The men I sent knew where he'd be and once they killed his bodyguards, how hard could it be to kill him? You just point the gun at him, pull the trigger, and the bullet does all the work. How hard is that? I'm getting a bad feeling about this. I want this job over and done with." At that moment, a man burst through the door.

"Boss, put on the TV, quick! It's about what happened to our guys," a third man announced as he stormed into the room.

Kurt, the boss, walked over to the television and flipped on a local station. A female newscaster was reporting. The lower third of the screen read: BLOODY SHOOTOUT ON SECOND AVENUE.

"Early this morning, they found four men shot and killed by unknown gunmen. Witnesses report that three men entered the restaurant and ordered everyone to the rear of the store. Their intended victim was a customer in the Good Burger restaurant in midtown Manhattan. But, witnesses and police say three shots fired from an unknown shooter prevented that. The shooter killed all three gunmen, and they found a fourth man dead from a gunshot wound in what police say appears to be the getaway car parked in front of the restaurant. The police questioned customers and workers who were present, but the shooter appears to be a mystery. Whoever he or she is, it was apparent that this person saved the lives of a young man and perhaps the remaining restaurant's occupants. Our mystery shooter is being hailed as a hero. The gunmen's primary target seemed to be this young man of approximately twenty to twenty-five years of age, possibly linked to the murder of several men near the United Nations building and the missing king of Talvania. The witnesses questioned by the police claim there were three quick shots fired from what seemed to be inside the restaurant, killing the three gunmen. But the puzzle here is that no one could say who fired the shots. The police searched the restaurant and its patrons for weapons, but they found none. Initial tests show that there was no paraffin residue or traces of gunpowder found on any of the restaurant's occupants. Apparently, a gunman raised his gun to this young man, the intended target. Just as he was about to be shot, at that precise moment, an unknown shooter killed the three gunmen. This is a puzzling case, police say, and they are asking anyone who may have any information to call police headquarters." The journalist looked straight into the camera, paused for effect, and in a somber voice said to the viewing audience, "Remember Bernie Goetz? Well, we may have another vigilante among us, folks... once again... in our city."

"Sonofabitch. That bastard must have had backup bodyguards that we knew nothing about or else he had a gun on him we weren't told about," Kurt said angrily.

"What do you want us to do, boss?"

"Call all our men. I want everyone out on the street. I want you to find this kid!"

"But we don't know where to start," one man responded.

"Start at the restaurant! Ask questions! Check the stores! He couldn't have gotten far in this weather," he yelled, his voice getting louder and louder. "He has to be somewhere close and he must walk because no one's crazy enough to drive a car in this weather but us. Go!"

Lom opened the door to his small apartment. The room had warmed up a bit. He could now exhale and not see his breath. The snow on the windowsill and door had acted as a seal, he surmised. Once again, he turned on all the stove burners and the oven. It was still cool in the apartment, but it was tolerable. He placed water into a pot and set it onto the stove, then realized that he had once again forgotten that he had no coffee left. They'd have tea, instead, he told the kid. Each took a seat at the opposite end of a tiny wooden table. The old man looked at the kid. For a moment, he saw himself at this age, only his hair back then was black and the kids were blond.

"You want to tell me about it?" Lom asked.

"The communists are trying to get rid of me to accomplish their goal of taking over my country. My brother might send his men, or how you say, mercenaries, from my country to kill me, but they are unfamiliar with this City of New York. So, they have planned with killers from your country. I'm sure that some serious money was involved in finding and kill me. They scheduled me to speak at the UN this morning, but they ambushed us as we were getting out of the car. They murdered my bodyguards, but in the confusion, I escaped. I ran as fast and as far as I could. I was lucky because the heavy snowfall helped me—they could not see me. That's the only reason I escaped. I ran and hid in a doorway and when I saw them in a car in front of the restaurant, I was sure they had seen me. When they drove away, I knew they hadn't, so I felt safe inside the restaurant because surely they would not return to the same place. I was wrong. They would have killed me if you were not there. Thank you."

"Explain to me once again what you were doing here?"

"I was to speak at UN. I want support from them."

"Hell, son. The United Nations won't help you! They're nothing but useless, self-serving, condescending, irrelevant, self-impressed bastards! They wouldn't help you unless there was something in it for them. That's just my opinion, but what do I know?" Lom did not hold the UN in high regard. His words were surprising to the young man. Torbjorn ran his hands through his hair and then put his hands on both cheeks and looked up with sad eyes.

"I don't know what to do. I'm alone in a strange country– no friends, no money and, to tell the truth, I'm scared. Thank you again."

"Well, you're wrong about one thing, son."

"Okay."

"You said you don't have any friends here, but you do now. You have me. We'll take it as it comes. If I'm any judge of men, they'll be back. They'll question the people at the restaurant and someone will tell them about me. I'm a regular there and sure as there's a moon above, they'll be here soon."

"What do we do?" the King asked nervously.

"I know of a place where we'll be safe, at least for a little while. Then we'll figure a way to get you back home where you can kick some country ass. Before we leave, though, I need to know what name your friends call you."

The young king smiled and said, "My friends call me Toby."

"Toby, huh? That sounds American. Well, I have to say I like that name, Toby. It sorta fits you. Okay, Toby it is. Take your jacket off and put these on," he said as he handed him his lumber jacket and spare cap. "Pull the cap down over your face. Everyone will think you're wearing it that way because of the cold, but it'll disguise your face, you know, cover the face, so they won't recognize you." Lom went to his bureau. He opened a box of forty-five caliber shells, grabbed an extra magazine, and replaced the bullets. He took the other two magazines that were lying in the drawer and slid bullets into them. Next, he opened his footlocker next to the bureau, took out a Randall fighting knife, and strapped it to his thigh. He had carried this knife all throughout the war. He hid it in his long winter coat. Toby watched with interest as Lom went through the ritual of replacing the bullets in his clips. "Where did you learn to shoot like that?" he asked.

"Three tours in Korea, son. I was a Ranger. The Rangers patrolled, scouted, ambushed, and destroyed the Communist Chinese and the Korean enemies. The 1st Rangers—that's the company I was in — wiped out the 12th North Korea Division headquarters in a night raid. I was the top marksman, if I say so myself, both with a rifle and this old 1911 Colt forty-five. My M-1911 here is a single-action, semi-automatic, magazine-fed, recoil-operated handgun chambered for the forty-five ACP cartridge."

This was all dizzying to the King—too many adjectives that were hard to follow. Lom knew his weapons, and he derived great pleasure from discussing them.

Lom continued, "I carried this gun for three tours in Korea and took it with me when I returned home. The clip holds seven rounds and with one in the chamber, that gives me eight rounds. The two other two clips have seven as well, bringing it to a grand total of twenty-two rounds. Now, if I can't hit what I'm aiming at with twenty-two rounds, I might as well use the last bullet on myself." He laughed. "I know there are other guns out there that hold ten and even twenty rounds like that Hershel FN5.7, but if you know how to shoot, you only need a few rounds to do the job. Like what happened this morning. This gun has stopping power. That's what I needed in Korea and that's what I want in civilian life. I never wanted to use this gun because of the stupid gun laws in New York City. Normally, I would just toss any of my used weapons, if you get my drift," he said as he winked, "into the East River, but not this one—I love this gun. This is my baby. It was with me all those years in Korea and it has never let me down. When I look at it, I see an old, reliable friend. I would never part with an old, reliable friend, be it human or otherwise. I carry it with me every day and... What would have happened if I had left it at home today?" Toby nodded in agreement, knowing that the old man had saved his life. Toby was glad, too. Lom added, "I hope I won't have to use it again, but if I do, it won't be pretty. I don't miss when I shoot." Lom looked at his watch and waited a little while before leaving. Charlie would open his shop in a few minutes and he wanted to give him a heads up in case anyone came looking for him. He had the key to the store and could let himself in, but he preferred to wait for Charlie. Besides, waiting was good. They could shorten the time they needed to get where they needed to decrease their chances of being seen. The stall time might work for them.

At seven a.m., Lom heard the bell tinkle as the door to the pawnshop opened. It was the sign that Charlie had arrived. Lom walked to a door hidden behind a curtain in the room's corner and knocked twice. They locked the door from the pawnshop's side. Lom preferred it that way. Charlie opened the door and was just about to ask why Lom didn't walk around to the front of the store and let himself in, as he usually did, but was a little surprised to see a stranger standing beside him. Lom didn't have too many visitors.

"Come on in. Don't just stand there like some goddamned, no-account dummy." This was Charlie's way of saying, "glad to see you."

"Who's that you have with you?" Charlie asked.

"Charlie, I want you to meet a friend of mine. Say hello to Toby."

"Hi Toby. Nice to meet you, but you can't be too smart to be hooked up with this ornery old coot." Toby smiled and said nothing. He was a little shy and still unsure what the pawnshop, Charlie, and this introduction had to do with him.

The men entered Charlie's office, where it was nice and warm. It reminded Lom of his cold flat. "Look, Charlie, before we get started…"

"Yeah?"

"My apartment is freezing. I had to put on the oven and the burners on the stove just to keep from freezing and that's not the safest thing, ya know, leaving on a gas stove, but I had to just to get it slightly warmed up."

"Sorry about that," Charlie responded. "It must be that old thermostat acting up again. I'll check it out. It's not right not to have heat on such a snowy night. I'll have it fixed before you come home."

Lom paused for a moment, and then proceeded, "That's just it, Charlie. I may not be coming home, at least for a little while. I would have left earlier, but I wanted to warn you about something. If anyone comes looking for me, don't lie. Tell them anything they want to know. If they want to see my room, let 'em in and show it to 'em. Let 'em see it."

"Lom, what on earth happened? What did you go getting yourself into now?" Charlie asked, knowing that Lom always had a bit of a mischievous streak.

"Did you listen to the news this morning?" Lom asked.

"Well," Charlie said. "I always put on the news when I'm in my car, only I didn't take my car this morning. Too much snow. I took the subway instead. Why? What happened?"

"It's a long story, but the short of it is, I killed four men this morning at the diner and some terrible people might come knocking on your door. I just wanted you to be prepared, that's all." Charlie stared at his friend, giving him an incredulous smirk. He rolled his eyes and turned to arrange some of the new stuff that pawners had brought in. When he turned back around, he saw Lom wasn't smiling. He seemed serious.

"What the hell? You ain't smiling Lom. Toby, why ain't he smiling?"

"Because, it's true. I was there," Toby replied.

"Oh, okay. You tell me this early in the morning, before I've had my coffee, I might add, that you shot up the diner and killed four men. And on top of it, say, 'That's all'?" Charlie said sarcastically. "You went and killed four men and all you can say is 'That's all'? Damn Lom, why did you kill four men? What in the hell did you do that for?"

"They were about to kill Toby here and I just couldn't let that happen."

"Of course you couldn't, Lom," Charlie replied sarcastically. "You're getting too frigging old for this kind of nonsense. What are you going to do if they find you?"

"I'll just have to kill 'em. I may have to find them myself, and that's what I'll do if I'm not given any other choice," Lom answered.

"Of course you will, Lom. It's what any normal person does. They go hunting people who are hunting them and they just… kill them. Kill every one of them. They just shoot them wherever they are. You are one crazy sonofabitch."

Charlie looked at Toby and said, "Me and Lom served in Korea together. It was me that got him that Silver Star they pinned on him. They wound me bad, and if Lom hadn't come to get me, the enemy would have and I'd be dead for sure. But he came for me. This crazy man caught a bullet in the back because of it, because of me." Charlie's voice cracked a little as his eyes slightly misted. He continued, "Back then, nobody would mess with him. Anything he shot at, he killed. If you picked a fight with him, you might as well be tugging on Superman's cape because Lom would fight to the end. Somebody was going to get hurt... and usually, it was the other guy." He turned and looked directly at Lom. "But look at you now. You're a crotchety old man who can't fight his way out of a paper bag and if you fell to the ground, you couldn't get that crinkly old body up fast enough to defend yourself. Geez. Now I won't be able to sleep until I hear from you again."

"Don't you worry any about me, Charlie. I may not be agile anymore and, like you say, I may not get myself up off of the floor quick anymore, but I can still shoot the eye out of a fly at a hundred yards."

Charlie nodded. "You're right there. The good Lord gave you that ability and He never took it away from you. He took away your youth and your fighting skills, but He didn't take your eyesight 'cause you can still see twenty-thirty at your nimble old age, and he didn't take away your ability to handle a gun. Maybe he has another purpose for you in this lifetime. Maybe it's helping Toby here—I don't know. Although why he would want a mean, cantankerous pain-in-the-ass like you to do, it is beyond me. But who knows the ways of the Lord? Not me, that's for sure. Okay, so if these guys come looking for you and they stop in my store, I'm to tell them whatever they want to know. Am I right so far?"

"Yeah, so far," Lom replied.

"Okay, then go on and tell me the rest," Charlie insisted. "And if they ask if you live here, I'm to tell 'em the truth?"

"Yeah, you tell 'em anything they want to know."

"Okay, I tell 'em you live in the room behind the store and I open the door and show 'em your room. Man, my friend, you are damn crazy—suicidal!"

"No, don't open the door from inside the store. Give 'em the key and let 'em go outside to get into my room. You never can tell if one day we'll need that secret entrance for something. Ya got that?"

"Yeah, yeah, I got it. But do you really think they'll find out that you're living here?"

"I don't rightly know, Charlie. What I know is this young fella here is a mighty important man in his own country and the people who are after him will do anything to find him, it appears, and that includes killing him. And I just won't allow that to happen. Not as long as I have a breath left in this old body of mine. You understand what I'm saying, Charlie?"

Charlie sighed and nodded. Yes, he knew. He had known this crazy bastard for a long time and this was the same crazy bastard who had saved his life. He had cared then more about someone else than he did his own safety and this was just history repeating itself.

Lom continued, "Now, please close this place down for a week and maybe go to Florida and look at some pretty girls in bikinis. I say you should 'look' at them, because at your age you sure as hell won't be able to do anything else with them." He chuckled.

"Hilarious, Lom. No, I don't close my shop for nobody. At my age, I won't run from nobody, either. So if they see fit to shoot this wreck of a body, then so be it."

"I wish you'd change your mind, Charlie. You're the only friend I have left in the entire world. Be real careful. Watch out for anything unusual. You hear me, Charlie?"

Charlie said nothing, but began walking toward the shop's counter. "Come over to the counter a minute. I want to give you something," he said as he pulled a box from a shelf under his counter. "Take this with you."

Charlie opened the box and took out a Glock twenty-two. "Take this, Lom. It has three fifteen-round clips–forty caliber." Charlie then opened the cabinet behind him and pulled out a box of forty-caliber ammunition, loaded the clips, and rammed a clip into the gun. He pulled back the receiver and chambered a round. He then pulled the clip back out and inserted another nine-millimeter round into it. "It'll stop someone almost as good as your old nineteen eleven Colt. And take this radio. Call me along the way and let me know your whereabouts. Let me know you're safe. I think I know where to reach you. Anything after that? Keep me posted, you hear?"

Lom looked at the gun and then looked at Toby. "You take the gun, Toby. You shouldn't be walking around naked. Take the gun and the other two clips and, while you're at it, take that box of ammo too. I'll take the radio. That all right with you, Charlie?" Lom asked.

"Here, take it. It's my gift to you," Charlie said as he handed the gun to Toby. Charlie then walked over to the door and pulled down the shade so no one could see inside the store. He walked over to a rug on the floor and pulled it aside, revealing a grid. The metal cover was about two feet square. Charlie lifted the grid from the floor. "Come on and get down there now before a customer walks in."

Toby looked confused. "What's down there?"

"Safety, my boy. Safety is what's down there," Charlie assured him.

"You best be going now," Charlie insisted. "If these men are looking for you and they show up here, I don't want you getting blood all over my tidy store and dying here in my office."

"Thanks, Charlie. Hey, if you decide to come visit, bring us some food, okay? I'll call ya along the way, when it's safe," Lom said.

Charlie responded, "Yeah, I'll do that. I'll try to bring you some supplies and food and stuff. Take care."

The two men stepped onto the narrow ladder that took them a long way down into total darkness. Toby trusted Lom, especially after watching him save his life, so he obediently followed close behind. It was a long way down to who knew where. When they reached the bottom and stepped off the ladder, they stood in a dark tunnel in front of some train tracks.

The workers who built the subways built a shortcut in an empty lot to make it easier for them to get to work. In time, the entrance was lost and forgotten. Charlie bought an old condemned home from the city and while he was tearing it down and ripping out the foundation to make room for the pawnshop he planned to build, he discovered the grid covered by the concrete foundation. Before covering the opening, he investigated where it led. After stepping down the ladder and following the tracks in both directions, he made some important discoveries. He decided the grid was worthwhile saving. He built his pawnshop right over the ancient unused and all-but-forgotten entrance to the subway tunnels, making sure that it remained hidden, but was easily accessible from within his store.

Lom did not know if they used these rails. "Come on. Stay close to the wall and let's try to get to where we're going before a train comes by."

Toby asked, "And just where is it we're going? I'm just following you, Lom, and do not know what's going on."

"Just hang with me, King. You'll see. We just need to hide for as long as we can."

They walked through the dark tunnel. Dim lights spread a ghostly yellow haze for about a city block. Underneath their feet, they felt the tracks vibrate and, in the distance, there was the light from a train fast approaching. Instinctively, Lom pulled Toby toward him and backed them into what appeared to be a worker's alcove while the train thundered by. At that moment, Toby let out a yelp. "Whoa! Did you see that? Look, Lom. It's a beast!" Lom laughed until he could hardly breathe. "Tunnel rats," he said amid gasping for breath between his guffaws.

"Tunnel rats?" Toby repeated as he stood fixated in the alcove, too afraid to move. "Mr. Lom, as a ruler, I must study history. You are playing with me. Tunnel rats were in the war. Tunnel rats are men."

"Wow," Lom answered. "I'm impressed there, King. You know how many people don't know what a tunnel rat is? Yeah, you're right. They were soldiers in the Vietnam War. Huh. You know that? I guess it's because that war is still so fresh in everyone's mind. Wonderful stuff. Yeah, but these here 'beasts' are rats. New York City is full of 'em. They can grow to over a foot long. Nasty creatures, but they love the subway tunnels." And at that moment, an entire pack of them assembled up and down the tracks. Toby winced. He knew rats, but he had never seen ones as big as these.

Another train passed, causing the rats to scurry. Lom hopped down and walked alongside the track as sure-footed as a billy goat. Toby stayed behind him. A few minutes passed until Lom spotted the steps. He motioned for Toby to follow and together they walked up the concrete stairs into an old abandoned train station.

Toby had those in his country and at a moment's notice, his staff could swoop him down into the ground to protect him from... whatever. Toby noted the faded posters still stuck to the walls, one with a fierce look and a finger pointing directly at him, proclaiming "Uncle Sam Wants You!" Toby followed Lom along the lengthy concourse, past stores that were dirty and abandoned. For a while, he said nothing, too ensconced in the history surrounding him, but finally, Toby asked, "What is this place?"

"They built this station to handle the traffic that World War II generated. We're right at the Forty-Second Street Broadway Station. After the war, it was no longer needed—closed down and they haven't used it since then. There are a few stations like this one, closed. They built one for the first World's Fair in nineteen thirty-nine. When the fair ended, the station was unused until the second World's Fair in nineteen sixty-four. And it brought the bridges and the streets back to life again. Who knows? Maybe someday it'll be reborn again. Come on. It's just a little farther up the ramp. Try not to be seen. There's a gate running across the back of this station that nobody uses, but people use the station on the other side of the gate. Make sure no one sees you."

The men walked by a recessed door standing between two plate-glass windows. The windows originally were there to display the store's merchandise. Lom reached into his trouser pocket and took out a set of keys. He searched through them, finding the key he needed, inserted it into the lock, and opened the door. He reached into his back pocket and removed the cumbersome flashlight that he had stored there and clicked it on. The men made their way to the rear of the store, where Lom opened another door and stepped into a modestly furnished room. He closed the door behind him, hit a switch, and light immediately flooded the room. Toby could see tarps covering several objects. Lom removed the first tarp. Underneath was a table with two chairs. Next, he uncovered a cot against the wall and a stove in the corner by the sink. The King walked over to the sink and turned on both faucets. To his delight, there was both hot and cold running water. He shot Lom a puzzled look. "Lom, how did you get light, water, and a bathroom working in this store that's been closed almost sixty years?" he asked.

"Charlie. Charlie discovered this little place. He brought me down here one day to see it. We decided it might be nice to make one of these stores livable with a few needed amenities. I guess it's like a kid having a secret hide-a-way. We rationalized it, calling it our little bomb shelter. Who knows? Everybody needs a safe place, right? Especially with nuclear weapons and such." Toby nodded in understanding. Lom continued, "Charlie's real handy. He knows about plumbing and electricity and he hooked it up and got the bathroom working and don't ask me how he did it, because I couldn't tell you. He had to tap into pipes or something somehow. We put down the tarps, never knowing when we'd return. If we hadn't, we'd be spending all of our time cleaning and dusting. It's dirty enough as it is, but at least we covered the most important things. I'm glad to see everything still works because I haven't been down here for at least two years… but I sure am glad we had the foresight to do this. Amazin' that these pipes never froze up. Charlie made a key for the store. In fact, he made keys for a few of the stores, but we haven't really explored those yet. Just opened the doors to make sure that the keys work. We chose this one because it's back far enough from where the trains pass, and close enough that if we had to make a run for it, we could open the gate over there and make our getaway through that station. Pretty neat, huh?"

"Neat?" Toby asked. "Not neat. Dirty, to tell the truth."

Lom laughed. "It's just an expression. No, it's not really neat, but it's, uh, it's cool."

"Cool, yes. It's a little cool. I like cool more than hot."

"Never mind, King," Lom smiled. "Sometimes English just makes little sense."

Cool was right, but it wasn't as cold in this abandoned train station as it was in Lom's room. Maybe it was because it was far enough below the Earth's surface that the cold couldn't really bite into you. It didn't matter, though, because years ago, Charlie had brought two electric heaters to the room and left them here for a rainy day.

"Lom, can I ask question?"

"Sure."

" Why did you help me? You shoot men and take me to your home. You don't have to help me. Why are you doing it? Why bring me here now?"

"Toby, I spent thirty-five years serving my country.—three were in Korea fighting those communist bastards from the start of it to the end. To be exact, June 27, 1950 'till we signed the armistice on July 27, 1953. First two years, I was a private, but they discharged me with the rank of Master Sergeant. I believed in it. Believed in what we fought for even when school kids spat at us and called us baby killers. Yep, called us baby killers, just as they did later when men returned from fighting in Vietnam. That's the forgotten war son, the Korean War, the war nobody remembers, the soldiers nobody acknowledges. I was in some pretty historical battles—the Battle of Dien Bien Phu in Vietnam, the Battle of Chosin Reservoir, where we fought a brutal seventeen-day battle in freezing weather, as well as... the Inchon Invasion. I was with General Douglas MacArthur when he masterminded that extremely effective amphibious assault against the North Koreans in Inchon Harbor. Within two weeks, we destroyed the North Korea army. All of us fighting men were proud of what the General did in that assault. The commies were pushing us around pretty bad by the commies and during our retreat, the General took us out in boats where we swung around the enemy lines, landed right behind them, and took the North Korea army by surprise. We were fighting the Chinese army then, not the North Koreans, like everyone believed. General MacArthur wanted to take his army right into China and finish it, just like General Patton wanted to fight the Russians at the end of World War II. Oops! There I go again. You got me started. Sorry, I get a little sidetracked sometimes. Let's see, what was the question? Oh, you wanted to know why I'm helping you. I'll tell you why. I'll fight for the little guy any day of the week. And if you know it, even though you may be somebody important in your country, to me, you're still the little guy, and if I can help it, I won't sit by and allow anyone to hurt the little guy. Now, does that answer your question?"

"Yes, I guess," Toby answered, still a bit confused by it all. One thing for sure was that Toby knew his history and even though Lom had a way of being long-winded, Toby recognized certain facts and timeframes that Lom referenced. Toby was admiring the old man, who took so much pride in his country and in defending it. That was what every leader of any country wanted—men and women who were loyal.

"Well, I have my question for you, King Toby."

"Okay. Ask."

Lom, with his nose crinkled a bit and his eyes crunched together in wonder, asked, "Why don't you just call home and have 'em fly a plane over here and get you?"

"Can't do that, Lom. The only person I trust right now is my head of security, Kari Swenson. No one else."

"Well, why don't you call him?"

"I can't take the chance. I suspect the phones at palace are—what do you say—'hit' and my words are being heard."

"Tapped," Lom corrected him.

"If I call him now, I'll tell the enemies where to find me. No, I must find another way to get home," he said matter-of-factly. This was the first time Lom had seen anything close to a stern quality in the King. He liked that. Lom was all about forceful character.

"If that's all that's troubling you, I think I can help," Lom chimed in.

"How? How can you help me get home?"

"You just leave it to me. But never mind that now. We have more important things to worry about at the moment."

Chapter Four

All eyes were riveted to the big-screen television as the same female news commentator they had heard earlier described the shooting of the four men at the Good Burger restaurant on Second Avenue. "The police questioned everyone at the restaurant at the time of the shooting," the woman said, "except for the intended target of the gunmen—a young man, and an elderly man who apparently left right after the shooting. The police are looking to question both of them and are asking anyone who knows their whereabouts to call police headquarters."

"Did you hear what she just said?" Kurt asked. "There was an old man there, and you guys missed him. Check with the people that work at the store and question them! See if they know him. He may be a regular. It's kind of strange that the kid and the old man go missing at the same time. I bet if we find the man, he'll lead us to the kid, or maybe we'll find him with the kid. Find that old man and bring him here! Do not, I repeat, do not kill him! We need to find out what he knows. Now go find him."

Toby jumped as Lom's military radio beeped. Lom picked it up from the table and pressed the button. "I'm here. Open the door. I brought you dinner," a voice said. Lom walked to the door, pulled the latch back, and opened it. There stood the best friend anyone in the world could have, holding a big bag of fried chicken, French fries, a six-pack of beer, and a tin of Maxwell House coffee. Lom and Toby suddenly realized how hungry they were. They had forgotten that they really hadn't eaten since their breakfast was so rudely interrupted by gunmen. Between bites, Charlie said, "They were back to the restaurant. They know who you are, Lom. They were pretty persuasive. These guys ain't fooling around. They questioned Martha. She didn't want to do it, but they were hurting her, so she caved. She told them about you. They even threatened her family if she didn't co-operate. They warned her not to tell anyone about their visit, saying they'd come back and hurt her for real. She came straight over to the pawnshop to tell me and asked me to warn you. I told her I'd pass on the information. I didn't want to leave the shop for fear of running into those guys, so I asked Martha if she would be so kind as to do me a favor and bring over some chicken, so I wouldn't have to leave. Told her I had to feed someone. Didn't tell her who, so if those guys came back, she'd be protected. Martha's sharp, so I think she figured it out when I said 'a lot of chicken.' I think she felt she let you down by spilling the goods on you. As soon as she brought the food, I thanked her and told her she'd better be going in case those boys visited me. They might put two and two together. She wanted to make sure you knew she didn't tell them where you live, but just that you sit in her section a lot. Didn't say too much more. Both she and I figured it won't be long before someone, maybe someone at the restaurant that you talked to in passing, tells them where you are. As soon as the door behind her closed, I locked up and skedaddled over here. I made sure the rug covered the opening real good. I wouldn't be surprised if I get a visit sometime soon after they snoop around some more. What do you think I should do, Edgar?"

Charlie only called Lom "Edgar" when he was nervous, angry, scared, or tired, and right now, he was a little bit of all.

"Do you still have that contact at the telephone company?"

"Yeah. He's my sister's kid."

"Well, I can only think of two things you can do. One—you can stay here with us until this thing blows over. Or two—you can go back to your shop and when they come in, you can answer their questions and make them think you're mad at me for not paying rent for the last three months."

"But, Lom, you don't owe me any money for rent," Charlie said nervously.

"I know that, dingbat. It's just to make them think your sort of pissed off at me, you know, like I was a deadbeat or something. You could tell 'em that you want to find me just as bad as they do. Tell 'em to leave a number with you and you'll check around, and if you come up with anything, you'll call them. Make them think that you might have a way of finding me. Let them know that you'll have to track down some people who might help you. You can even reassure them by telling them they're welcome to check back with you if they don't hear from you in the next twenty-four hours. Now, as soon as they give you their phone number, you call your sister's kid at the telephone company and get me an address for that number. I'll do the rest."

"You sound pretty confident, Lom," Toby said.

This American could talk. Toby had heard no one talk so much when he asked them a simple question or made a comment. Lom was nowhere near finished. "When I ran out of ammunition for the fifty caliber, I picked up a B.A.R. (a Browning Automatic Rifle) and I fired that until it, too, was out of ammo, and when I looked for more of the rifle ammo, there was none, so then I fired whatever I could get my hands on. I don't remember the night leaving and the morning coming, but when there was light, I saw bodies up top of the bunker—some so close to me I could almost touch 'em. When help came, they counted three hundred and twenty-some-odd men that I killed that night, and you know what?"

"What?" Toby was afraid to ask, but did.

"I never saw one face of the men that I killed that night. Now, do you think that those tough guys could make me lose a night's sleep? Nah. Don't you worry about me. I may be old, but I can still take care of myself. And you want to know something else? If one of these bastards looking for you got in a lucky shot, they'd mostly be doing me a favor because I'm getting near the end of the road anyway, and being killed quickly by a bullet, that's the way to go out." He turned to Charlie. "Charlie, you just concentrate on getting me that phone number. And I'm thinking that after I go after them, maybe some others will come around asking you questions. I think it might do us some good if you gave them this place. But I'm getting ahead of myself. Let's take it one step at a time. First, we need to find out where they are. Later on, I'll have 'em come visit me right here. Yep. It's sounding like a plan. You got all that, Charlie?"

"Yeah, Edgar. I do."

Charlie left, but as he approached the door, Lom called out, "Hold on a minute, Charlie."

"What?"

"No, nothing's wrong. I just forgot to give you something, that's all. I must really be getting old. Damn, but I can't remember anything lately. I hope I'm not getting that old folk's disease where you can't remember anything anymore."

"What did you forget?" Charlie asked.

"I forgot to give you this." He handed Charlie the cell phone. He took off the dashboard of the Mercedes after he shot the driver. "See if your nephew can check this cell phone and get me the address off of this one. Must be a way. Who knows? We may get their home address and their business address. Tell him to check it out and when you get it, bring it here to me. I'll handle it from there. Be careful, Charlie, and thanks." Charlie nodded and then began his trek back through the tunnel. It was quiet for a moment.

Toby broke the silence and asked, "Why did Charlie call you 'Edgar'? Is Edgar your real name?"

"Yep. My real name's Edgar, and the only one I allow to call me that is Charlie. He does it when he's upset about something. Charlie's a fine man. Don't know how I'd live with myself if anything were to happen to him because of me, but yes, my real name is Edgar and don't you go getting any ideas that you can call me that too. I'm Lom and that's what you'll call me. Got it, King Toby?" With that, he smiled. He was an ornery old coot, just like Charlie said, talking to a King like that. Lom was Lom, royalty present or not. You had to love him.

"Of course. I'm pleased to call you as you wish. How'd you get the name 'Lom'?" he continued. Boy, Lom thought, once the boy started talking, he got on a roll. The King looked serious, and he was genuinely trying to learn more about Lom.

"Well, my last name is Lombardi. Ever since I was a kid, everybody has always called me 'Lom.' Now don't you go telling anyone my real name. You hear?"

Toby chuckled. "Don't worry, Edgar Lom. Your secret name is safe with me."

Lom looked at Toby to decide if he was being truthful. After a second or two of just staring at him, he said, "Okay. Now let's plan our next move."

"Before we figure out our strategy, I noticed that you have an accent," Toby commented.

"Funny, coming from you," Lom responded. "I noticed you have one, too." He chuckled.

"I can tell you're not a New York man. Where's your home, Edgar Lom?" he smirked.

Lom raised an eyebrow, then smiled. He was getting used to the King and the banter between them. It was entertaining. The King was growing on him. "I grew up in Pall Mall, Tennessee—home of Sergeant Alvin C. York. York, as in New York. Hmm... funny coincidence, fortuitous, maybe. Well, I grew up with a lot of young boys who could shoot a mite better than me. I think sharp shooting is in the genes of every man born there. I migrated to New York because of Charlie. Charlie was born in Missouri, but moved to New York after the war; he wanted to experience the big city. After Korea, he said his priorities changed, wanted to do something different. I had no family, no one to come home to after the war, and me and Charlie had become like brothers in Korea, so I did what he did. I went with Charlie. He had a few bucks from his family and loved guns and knives like me, so he decided that being a pawnbroker was the perfect career for him. Couldn't thank me enough for savin' his life, so… he offered to give me a room in the back. We get to see some pretty amazing memorabilia. Don't let that hound dog look on his face, fool you. When the chips are down, Charlie is as good a fighting man as you could ever find, but like me, he's getting old. Now, let's get to strategizin'."

Two days later, Charlie was busy placing his newly gained items into the glass cabinets. These items were now officially for sale—the ones that were pawned where the owners never returned to redeem them. Their time period had run out and now he owned them outright. There was a blue sapphire ring that he placed on a black tray with other rings. These had to be locked away. He placed an old silver cigarette case on an odds and ends shelf. He figured the item would probably sit there for a while, but eventually, someone, some collector, would recognize its value and buy it. It was a beautiful case, used in the nineteen forties, but cigarette cases were rarely, if ever, used today. He placed a one-carat engagement ring onto the "diamond" tray. A brokenhearted young lady had brought it in after her boyfriend had broken off their engagement and asked her to return it. Her response was not unlike others that Charlie had seen. She hocked it and she would angrily present her ex with a pawn ticket instead. The bell tinkled as the door opened and Charlie looked up to see three rough-looking men approaching him.

"Good morning, boys. What can I do for you?"

A large mean-looking man looked down at him and said, "We heard that you have an old man renting a room from you? Is that true?"

"Yeah. I sure rent a room to that moocher. At least I did until that sonofabitch took off without paying me my rent." Playing dumb, Charlie just waited until the mean man spoke again.

"Yeah. He owes us money too. Do you mind if we check out his place?"

Charlie paused a moment as if he were considering it.

"Sure. I can't see what harm that'll do. Maybe you'll find out something that'll tell both of us where that old bastard took off to. Man, I get some pretty rough, moral-lacking people that come to my business, but this one, I would have never figured he'd stiff me."

He led the men around the building to the outside door leading into Charlie's room and opened it for them. Everyone entered but Charlie. "Look, fellas, hope you don't mind if I leave you. Take your time and I'll be around the front. I got a store to look after. When you're finished in here, stop in with the key and let's talk. I have some ideas about where that old bastard might have gone."

The men appreciated the fact that they wouldn't have to use force to get this man's cooperation. The mean man said, "We'll be in as soon as we have a look around."

"Good. I'll see you when you're finished, then." And with that, Charlie turned and walked back into his store, smiling all the way. Welcome suckers, he thought. That ole coot of a friend was bringing back a little excitement into his life.

When the men returned to the store, Charlie tried not to look suspicious, so he kept busy arranging things on his shelves. The same man who asked the questions before approached Charlie and asked him to tell what he meant when he said he had some ideas about where the old man might have gone.

Charlie smiled and put out his hand and said, "I'm Charlie and since we might do some business together, I'd like to know what my partner's name might be."

It took aback the stranger a little. He had come here thinking he might have to hurt this guy and now this little man standing in front of him was smiling with his hand out, acting as if he was his partner in crime. He reciprocated by extending his hand and said, "I'm Chet. Now, what do you have for me?"

"Chet, I suggest you let me do some snooping around. I know a few places he used to frequent. There's an old chess emporium nearby. I'll ask around there and see if I can dig up some info on where he may have gone. There are some other places that I'll have to check out too, so why don't we do this? Give me a number where I can reach you and as soon as I have some information, I'll call you. But understand something— when you find that old man, I want to have my rent money paid to me first. Is that understood?"

Chet didn't like anyone giving him an order, but in this case, he readily agreed to Charlie's proposition. He had no intention of paying him a penny. All he wanted was to find the old man and the kid and get Kurt off his back. Chet, without hesitation, said, "Sure. You have a deal. When we find the old man, I'll make sure you get the rent money he owes you. Does that satisfy you?"

Charlie smiled and said, "Yep. It sure does, young fella. Now give me a number where I can reach ya and when I have something for ya, I'll give you a ring. If you don't hear from me by tomorrow late in the afternoon, then come by and I'll tell you what little I learned. If I have something important to tell you immediately, I'll call you right away. Okay?"

"Yeah. That'll do." Chet wrote a phone number on one of Charlie's cards and handed it to him. "You can reach me at this number day or night. If I don't hear from you by tomorrow afternoon, I'll be VERY disappointed," he said, stressing the "very."

"Now there's no need to be getting uppity, young fella. I'll do my best and don't forget that I want him as bad as you do. That sonofabitch owes me three months' rent and I want it."

Charlie gave his nephew, George, the phone number Chet had given him. Then he remembered the cell phone Lom had given him. He hit the power button and scanned the recent calls. There were two numbers that they had used frequently, and one of them was Chet's. The other number was different, so he gave that one to George as well. George asked him for a couple of minutes and placed him on hold. About five minutes later, George got back on the line with the addresses that belonged to the two phone numbers. Charlie thanked his nephew, hung up the phone, and hurriedly put on his winter garments. Once again, he made his way down the secret ladder and into the tunnel.

Chapter Five

Charlie handed Lom the slip of paper with the addresses on it. Lom looked at them, trying to decide which one he should visit first. The first one was in Lower Manhattan, Hudson Street; the warehouse district. One hundred years ago, they knew this section as Hell's Hundred Acres because they built the warehouses entirely out of wood. When a fire broke out in a building, an entire block burned down with it. In later years, sprinklers solved that problem and they contained the fires. The second address was in the old Murder Incorporated Greenpoint section of Brooklyn.

"Okay, we have two addresses. I decided that the first one I'm going to visit is the Hudson Street one. It's closer, and it could be a warehouse or an office building. I'll go there tonight. I'm going to pay these boys a nice little sociable visit, but I doubt I'll be a welcomed visitor. Damn, now that I think about it, I sure could use me a silencer. If they have any lookouts stationed outside the building, like I would do, then that means I'll have no choice but to take them out before I get inside the place. My old Colt nineteen eleven will make enough of a racket to wake the entire neighborhood up. I need a 'quiet' advantage before I go inside. This old thing isn't good for that."

"I have a gun with a silencer back at the pawnshop," Charlie volunteered. Lom looked at Charlie like he was crazy.

"Charlie! You do not have a gun with a silencer! Where in the hell would you get a gun with a silencer?"

"I have one, I tell you. I took it in pawn and the guy never came back to reclaim it. It's this presentation gun issued to an

SS Colonel in World War II. You know, those special forces in Nazi Germany. Wait right here. Ha, well, like you're going anywhere. Okay, I'll go get it and you can look to see if you can use it. If you can, it's yours."

A smiling Lom turned to Toby and said, "Don't you like when a plan comes together?"

Toby smiled back. "Yes, I watch American TV too, sometimes."

An hour later, Charlie was back with a large shopping bag he placed on the table. "It's all yours, Lom. Look."

Lom opened the bag and took out a wooden display case. He placed it on the table and reverently opened the cover. Inside, snuggled comfortably in the red velvet bottom of the case, was a Walther PPKS nine-millimeter Kurtz with two clips and a metal cylinder.

"Charlie was right. There's the suppressor, and look," he said, pointing to a gold nameplate. "They presented it to a Colonel Kessler of the SS and see, it's got the German Eagle on the slide and the barrel," he said excitedly. "And what I really like is that it's a nine-millimeter. Most of these guns came in a thirty-eight caliber model, which doesn't have the stopping power I want. From my experience, it would take a couple of well-placed bullets to stop a man with a thirty-eight. This nine-millimeter has more stopping power and was pretty rare at the time. BUT . . . it has a drawback."

"What drawback?" Charlie asked.

"It's nickel-plated, which means the gun could reflect light. I'd much rather have a regular blue patina on my gun, but I guess beggars can't be choosers. But aside from the nickel plating, this gun is perfect, Charlie. Gee, this is worth a lot of money. Are you sure you want me to have this? They have not fired it, and you know, and once I fire it, it'll lose a lot of its value."

"Lom, guns are for shooting people. That's what guns are for. Use it and don't worry about it. The only thing important to me is for you to get back safely. I don't want to lose the only friend I have."

"This'll give me a slight edge, Charlie, because now I can take out any guards they stationed outside the place without makin' that noise I was worried about. Then when I get inside, I'll use the body stopper—my old reliable nineteen eleven Colt forty-five," he said. Lom was really getting into this.

"Somethin' else, Lom. Martha's been asking about you. She knows I know where you're staying and she's really concerned. Martha's feeling guilty because she thinks she let you down when she told those guys that you come into the restaurant each morning at a certain time. She's a good girl, though. She told me she saw you shoot those guys, but she never told them you were the shooter."

"Good!" Lom said. "Let 'em think I'm just another old geezer who'll wet his pants when they come 'n get me. And that's an advantage I have that they don't know about. All they want me for is to give 'em any information I have about Toby here. And then, sure as shooting, they'll kill me."

"You don't know that for sure. They may just ask you a few questions and let you go," Charlie chimed in.

"In your dreams, Charlie. These kinds of men don't leave witnesses. Nah... they'll want to kill me all right. That may work to my advantage, too. Well, we'll just have to wait and see. I'll just have to let things play out for a while."

"What about Martha? Do you want me to bring her here?" Charlie asked.

"No. Are you kidding'? Maybe if we go to Plan B, you can. If we go to Plan B, we can have either have you or Martha let these guys know where I am, but I don't really want to get her too involved in this."

"Oh, but I'M dispensable. I get it. Your ole buddy here can get hurt, but not Martha," Charlie chided.

"Come on, Charlie, you stubborn ole goat. You seem to enjoy this. Bow out anytime, my friend. I can take it from here."

Charlie asked, "When did you say you're going to see these guys? Did I hear you correctly? Did you say you're going to see them tonight?"

"You heard right. I have the address, so I'll check out the building tonight. I'll take the train to the Hudson Street Station and walk the rest of the way. Then I'll just play it by ear. I may go inside tonight after checking it out, or maybe it'll be tomorrow when I go in. But if I get the chance to go in there tonight, then I will. Like I said, I'll just have to let things play out." Then he thought of Martha and how much he'd like to see her. He wanted to thank her for caring and for wanting to help. She shouldn't be feeling guilty about what she said to those boys, and he wanted to tell her so himself.

"Charlie, is Martha working tonight or is she taking some time off because of what happened?"

"She told me she needs the money and can't afford to take a night off, so she'll be working tonight, I suppose. You know… it's strange, because ever since the shooting at the restaurant, their business has doubled—morbid curiosity seekers, I guess."

"Well," Lom said. "Then I think I might surprise her and stop by."

Although it was no longer snowing, it was still blistering cold. Later in the night, the door to the Good Burger restaurant opened and Lom stepped into the warmth of the establishment. He sauntered over to his favorite booth. A stunned, open-mouthed Martha was watching the entire time. She practically threw down the tray packed with food and rushed right over to him.

"What are you doing here? Are you crazy? They might come for you at any moment," she said, clearly annoyed.

"Now, don't you worry any, Martha. I'll be just fine. These fellas don't scare me and, who knows, maybe they'll be a mite bit scared of me. Now, how about a cup of that fine black coffee of yours and a lightly toasted, buttered bagel? Don't have time for dinner, so the coffee and bagel will do me just fine."

Martha walked over to Lom's booth and sat down opposite him. "Those men came back and threatened me if I didn't tell them who you are. Lom, I had no choice. I had to tell them where you lived."

"Now, now Martha," Lom consoled her. "I don't want you fretting over nothing. I'm perfectly safe and I'm staying somewhere where they'll never find me, and I don't blame you one bit for telling them where I live. Don't feel bad because I woulda done the same thing if it was me in your position." Martha doubted that, but she felt better hearing him say it.

"Lom, I saw you kill those men and I don't think anyone else saw you do it, or they would have told the police. They deserved it and I sure didn't want to see them kill that young man, so I don't blame you for doing what you did. But I never knew you had it in you, that you could do such a thing—kill four men and not let it bother you."

"That's what combat does to a man, Martha. When you've seen as much death as I have, it leaves a man kinda cold, with no feelings. I saw a thousand men die in front of my eyes. And when you've killed as many men as I have, a few more bodies mean little. And there'll probably be more deaths before I'm through, Martha. Look, I have to go now, but I'll be in touch soon. You take care now, and don't you worry any about me, you hear?"

Martha watched as the old man shuffled out of the restaurant. She was glad to see him leave. Martha wanted him out of here and safe in case those horrible men returned. She liked Lom and maybe... a little more than she should. He was genuine—old, but genuine—and she worried about him. Her mind raced. She wondered if this old man could really be a match for the hardened men who were stalking him, stalking her. She smiled and shook her head. In a strange way, she felt relieved. She'd been riddled with guilt and seeing him and fessing up had lifted a weight from her shoulders. His calm demeanor had a soothing effect on her as well. She picked her tray back up and headed over to the table full of construction workers, apologizing the whole time for an "unexpected delay."

Charlie and Toby were waiting for Lom as he walked back into the store at the end of the abandoned station. The three men discussed how best to approach the building on Hudson Street. Charlie would remain behind, but Toby was adamant that they include him in the plan. He insisted on accompanying Lom. Lom, seeing the futility in arguing with him, reluctantly agreed. Lom was used to working alone, but for this job, Toby might come in handy.

Toby convinced Lom that he was proficient with a handgun. As king of his country, he explained, it was mandatory that he take basic training, qualifying in using handguns and rifles until they eventually classified him as an expert shot. It surprised Lom to hear that he was also qualified in a variety of automatic weapons such as the Russian AK-47, AKM, and the M16A2 rifle.

"Damn, King, you've been holding out on me!" Lom exclaimed. "Actually, if you're that good, it makes me feel a little better, like someone else is there, watching my back. Okay, let's get to it."

The two men checked their weapons to ensure they were operational. Lom took both his Colt and the German gun with the silencer attached to it and his Randall fighting knife. He felt naked without that knife. They bundled up and walked to the end of the empty, unused terminal. They stepped down the steps, walking alongside the tracks a short distance to the Forty-Second Street Station. There, they waited until they could slip into the station unnoticed. The downtown subway screeched to a stop, the doors flew open, and they boarded—just an old man and his grandson taking a ride on the downtown train.

The Government and Parliament of Talvania were conveniently located inside the Royal Palace, with the Government occupying the lower eastern part of the building. The King and the Royal Family of Talvania occupied the rest of the palace, which was considered the Royal House. It included the King and Queen, and the King's eldest son and his spouse. Since Toby's absence and because Toby was not married and had no offspring, his brother Lars was acting king. Every country has to have continuity in its leadership and government, and Talvania was no different. In the event of an emergency, or if the ruling King was away on state business for an extended period, or had taken ill, the next in line would temporarily assume the reins of government. The citizens of Talvania were oblivious to recent events and intrigue taking place inside the Royal Palace.

"Is there any news to report?" Lars asked.

"No, Your Majesty. There is no word from America."

"Come, Becker. Are you going to stand there and tell me you have no news to tell me? Nothing at all?" the King asked.

"Well, there is some news, but it is not the news I expected. I was hesitant to inform you until I had something more substantial."

"Well, come on. Let's hear it."

"The men we hired are most proficient in what they do. I vetted them before giving them the money. They are competent and completely ruthless, but they have run into a problem."

"And what would that be, Becker?"

"The men traced the King to a restaurant where they trapped him. Just as he was to be executed, a gunman fired shots, from an undisclosed location it seems, and shot and killed our three men, and when that happened, well, I am sorry to report that the King escaped during the confusion. They, the ones in charge of this mission, have men looking everywhere for him, but he is nowhere to be found. It seems he may have had an accomplice."

Becker was a little nervous, anticipating the temporary King's next question.

"And who would this accomplice be, Becker?" he asked in a stern, sarcastic voice.

"I'm told it was a much older man that helped the King escape, Your Majesty."

"An old man? An old man, you say? You're telling me that a really old man helped my brother escape? Did I hear you correctly?"

"That's right, Your Majesty. An old man. We know nothing about him, but it's hopeful that we may have some information about him today. The old man owes his landlord money, and the landlord is eager to get his money, so he is cooperating with our men in America to find him. I'm told he will have this information on the King's location within twenty-four hours."

"Might I remind you, Becker, that I am the King? I, and only I, am the ruler of Talvania, right now, and always. Stop addressing 'him' as King."

"Yes, Your Majesty. My sincerest apologies. Yes, you are the King."

Lars thought for a minute and then looked at Becker. "Becker, what is the latest on Swensen? Is he co-operating?"

"No, Your Majesty. He refuses. I have him confined to the smallest, most uncomfortable cell in the lower dungeon."

"Good! That will keep that interfering bastard quiet for a while. Call me when he has something to say. He probably has nothing to tell you of any importance. Make it clear to him he needs to recognize me as King and agree to support me. And as soon as you hear from our friends in America, I want to know about it immediately. Do you understand?" Lars picked up some papers from his desk and, with a condescending wave of his hand, said, "You may go now, Becker."

Lom felt like he was back in the cold mountains of Korea, reconnoitering the enemy camp. It was as he suspected–two men stationed outside the warehouse. With their collars pulled up high and their ski masks covering their faces, Lom and Toby marched deliberately toward the men, chatting and gesturing, exhibiting nothing suspicious. The two men guarding the entrance suspected nothing. It was cold and anyone with common sense would protect their faces. The guards simply observed the two men as they approached. Lom tightened his grip on the silenced Walther dangling by his side as he walked toward them, as if to make small talk. Before the guards could speak, he whipped out the gun and fired two quick shots. The little gun coughed twice and two men lay dead. Lom and Toby each grabbed a man and dragged him to the side of the building, into the thick brush where no one would see them.

They moved toward the building with stealth, checking carefully to see if they were in the clear. They walked quietly through the doors. Once inside, they heard the faint sound of voices and moved cautiously toward them. Lom assumed a position that gave him a good lookout. He could see everything–four men, sitting at a table, playing cards. A bottle of liquor and four small, filled glasses sat in the middle of the table. Lom was sure the liquor served two purposes–putting fire in their stomachs on this cold winter night, and indulging in the obligatory, sociable drinks during a friendly card game. Two of the men carried shoulder holsters, and a third man had one on his belt. A fourth man's back was to him, making it hard to identify a weapon. He whispered into Toby's ear to keep a lookout in the bathroom and other portals.

"Just keep a cautious eye out for anything out of the ordinary, but above all, watch my back," Lom whispered. Lom was silent for a long time. Satisfied that it was safe, he motioned for Toby to stay put and signaled toward Toby's gun. Toby nodded in understanding. Lom placed his Colt into his shoulder holster and removed the PPKS. He held the little gun at his side as he strolled boldly into the room.

The card game stopped. The room fell silent. Every eye trained on the old man with the lop-sided smile as he approached, his gun held high in the air.

"Hi, fellas. Don't mind me barging in like this. I didn't want to disturb your little card game, but I hear you boys are looking for me."

"What the hell are you doing here? How did you get in here? Max, get in here!"

"Max is probably not going to answer," Lom said as he smirked.

At that moment, one man forcefully shoved the table, sending cards and glasses soaring into the air. Glass shattered and alcohol fumes filled the air. The man went for his gun. Lom took aim and shot him in the heart area. Another man already had his gun cocked and was ready to fire. As quick as lightning, Lom leveled a shot to his head.

Two men remained. "What do you want?" one man asked.

"What do I want? Is that what you just asked? What I WANT is to know what you want. Why are you boys trying so hard to find me? What is it YOU want from ME? Tell me, please. I don't like being hunted. Personally, I like to hunt, but I hunt animals! I really don't take too kindly to people hunting people and I really don't like it when you threaten women. That really makes me mad. Shame on you! Don't you know what boundaries are? Hell, even the mob has boundaries. They never touched women and children."

One man spoke up. "It's not you we want. We want the kid. Just hand him over and we'll back off."

"Can't rightly do that because that young fella is a friend of mine now and I take offense when men like you try to hurt people I like. Take, for example, that nice waitress lady who works behind the counter at the eatery where your fellas found themselves dead. She's my friend, too, and if one of you hurt her, why I'd just as soon shoot you right in the head like I would a rabid dog? It wasn't one of you boys that was threatening her, was it?" The two men quickly shook their heads.

"No, not me," each answered, stepping on the other's words.

"No, I didn't think so. Now I'll make a deal with you guys. You tell me the name of your boss and I won't kill you. I'll just cripple you a little bit. Now, how's that sound? Do we have a deal?"

Silence prevailed. Realizing the danger, one man grabbed a large bottle, lifted the table upright, and rushed at Lom, slamming the bottle hard down hard on Lom's head, knocking him to the floor. Lom's gun clattered from his hand and skittered across the wet scotch-covered floor. The man quickly reached for his gun. Lom calmly reached under his jacket, pulled his Colt from his shoulder holster, and fired a shot, killing the first man. The second guy had his gun aimed right at Lom. He had a bead on him, right within his gun's sight, and was seconds from taking a shot and killing him when another shot rang out from across the room. The man holding the gun fell dead onto the floor, landing right on top of Lom.

Lom looked up to see Toby walk from the shadows, a smoking gun in his hand and a shit-eating grin on his face.

"I'm glad I was of some use to you," Toby said wryly.

"Thanks. You saved my worthless hide, shooting that man quick like that," he said as Toby pulled him off the floor. "I got a little careless there. Allowed myself to get knocked to the floor. You know, once I'm on the ground, I'm like a turtle on his back. I really have a hard time getting up. It's a real chore for me to do it. I know that gunman would have killed me sure as there's a God above, because I was powerless to prevent it. When I'm standing on my feet, I'm probably as good with a gun as any man alive, but once I'm on the floor, I'm like Superman, with a bag full of kryptonite in his pocket. I'm useless. And if it weren't for you, Toby, I'd be a dead man right about now. So for that, I have to thank you. Now let's search these boys and see what we can find. Who knows? They might have something we can use."

Toby and Lom searched each sock, each pocket, down to the men's underwear. They accumulated four guns, four wallets, and two passports.

"Look at the stamps on these passports, Toby. They're from your country. These guys have used the passports to go there to arrange the deal. They probably spoke with your brother."

"No," Toby said. "They would have spoken to Becker. He's the head of security for my brother."

"Well, it really doesn't matter if they spoke to your brother, or Becker, or whoever. Looks like we're just starting this little adventure of ours. Now do me a favor and go through the wallets and take out all the cash, credit cards, any papers, and make sure that the wallets are completely empty. We'll use the cash to buy tickets to get us to Talvania. Might as was well take the credit cards; might need those, too. Get that bag that the liquor came in and put everything in there. We don't want to leave anything with fingerprints. When the police find the bodies with no wallets, they'll think it was robbery or murder for profit, a gang killing a rival gang. Now let's see if we can find our shells. I'd hate to leave those here for the police."

They searched until they accounted for all the spent shells. Lom placed them into his pocket. They had a thorough look around, and Lom spotted a shovel beside the door. He grabbed that as well.

The shovel came in handy. Lom dragged it behind them and scraped the snow to remove any trace of footprints, even though, truth be told, Lom felt the footprints in the snow wouldn't have mattered. But why take a chance? Once down the block, he laid the shovel beside a door. Nothing suspicious. It looked as if that tenant was using the shovel to remove snow from the path leading to his door. The two men walked to the subway and took it to Forty-Second Street. Still aware of every stranger and every movement, they cautiously waited before descending the steps and disappeared into the darkness of the tunnel.

Once back inside their underground haven, Lom turned on the lights and went straight to the coffeepot, preparing a fresh pot of his favorite–Starbucks white mocha. He had scolded Charlie for that Maxwell House and Charlie, the faithful friend, had replaced it. This little two-burner portable stove was nothing of an appliance, but it did the trick. Lom took the radio from his pocket and clicked it twice. That was the signal to Charlie that it was him. Charlie clicked the button. "Charlie here."

"Charlie, we're back. Can you bring us something to eat?"

"Sure. I'll pick up something and bring it over in a little while."

"Good. I have a few things here that I'd like to show you. Toby and I have a little collection of artifacts, let's say."

"I'm sure you do, Lom. I'm sure you do," Charlie said and signed off.

Toby and Lom made good use of their time. They began disassembling their guns, cleaning and oiling them, all the while making small chat.

"You ever hear of Wild Bill Hickok?" Lom asked.

"Sure. I think everybody in the world's heard of him," Toby proudly answered.

"Did you know Wild Bill Hickok would take the wads out of his guns every morning because even though they would most likely fire perfectly, he didn't want to take the chance that moisture from the dampness of the previous night might have gotten into them? So, he changed wads every morning, just to be safe."

Toby asked, "What's a wad?"

"Back then, Wild Bill used a Colt eighteen fifty-one black powder navy pistol, back when they didn't have full metal jacket bullets yet. They used paper wads that contained gunpowder and a ball. Wild Bill was a true marksman. He could have been a circus shooter with his accuracy. He used to give demonstrations that served a double purpose. It entertained people, but it also showed everybody what kind of shooter he really was. He carried regular Colts for everyday use, but for demonstrations or when he dressed up, he wore his ivory-handled eighteen fifty-one nickel-plated navy Colts."

The men meticulously reassembled their guns. Lom checked the pot of coffee. It was percolating. He wanted to have it ready when Charlie arrived. He heard his radio beep and clicked the button. "Lom here."

"Open the door. It's me, Charlie." Toby greeted him.

"Come on in, Charlie," Lom said as he poured the sweet-smelling brew. "Warm your old bones up. I got an entire pot waiting for you."

"Man, I can sure use it. It's freezing out there. Here, take this bag of food from me. I can't feel my fingers right now."

Toby and Lom recounted the evening's activities, taking turns to fill in the blanks for Charlie.

"Man, Lom, that makes eight men you killed," Charlie said. It wasn't clear by his tone if it impressed or shocked him.

"Well, that's not exactly true, Charlie. Toby here killed one man and a good thing he did because I was just about to get it."

"You know exactly what I mean," Charlie continued. "Eight guys are dead and do you think the guy in charge is going to stand by and just be embarrassed and all?" There was silence. "Well, do you?"

"No, I guess he won't. I know I wouldn't take it lying down if it was me. I'd want the guys who killed my men, and I'd want them bad."

"Well, I've been thinking about this and I think it's about time you got out of town for a while. Don't you?" Charlie asked.

"Hell no! I ain't going nowhere, Charlie. The fun is just starting. This may be just the break I was looking for. I think maybe it's time Martha should let the men who contacted her know where to find me. It'll get them off her back and keep her safe. Or maybe we get real lucky and they'll come to your place again. Just keep letting them know how pissed off you are about my skipping out on the rent, and then, if you feel the time is right, then tell them where I am. But do not, under any circumstances, go with them. Use your gun if you have to, but do not get into a car with any of them. Once you're in the car, it's over. Now look at what we have here." Lom pulled out the bag and dumped everything on the table. "Toby and me took these from the guys we killed. There are four guns here. I want you to take them. Have your contact with the police run the serial numbers. If any come back as used in a crime, then throw those in the river. If the guns come back clean, then put 'em on the shelf in the display case in your store and sell 'em. Now, Charlie, don't be afraid to use one of 'em if you have to."

"Oh, come on, Lom. Don't keep treating me like a beginner. I carried a gun and shot and killed men just like you did, so don't go tellin' me what to do with a gun, understand? For heaven's sakes, I'm a pawn broker. I've been around guns for years."

"Okay, okay, don't take offense. I meant nothing by it," Lom quickly cut in.

"I know you're just worried that something will happen to me," Charlie said. "And don't worry, I won't let myself get killed by getting in somebody's car. I won't allow that to happen–me getting killed. I would hate having you coming to my funeral and me lying in my casket, all dressed up in my new suit, looking nice and all, and you standing over me cussing me out about how stupid I was getting in some stranger's car after you finished tellin' me not to. No, I won't give you the satisfaction of tellin' me that. You just take care of those guys and get this young man back home."

"Well, that's the next thing I want to talk to you about. You still have those guys that keep coming into your shop buying stuff and always asking you for credit card numbers? You know, those scammers?" Lom asked.

"Yeah," Charlie said, shaking his head. "They keep asking me for credit card numbers, I keep tellin' 'em no, but they don't give up. They know I'm legit, but ever since that business deal, the one we did with the jeweled twelfth century dagger that we all made a ton of money on, they keep coming back. I think Sydney Greenstreet likes me."

"Sydney who?"

"Victor. He looks just like Sydney Greenstreet, the old movie actor, the one who starred in THE MALTESE FALCON with Humphrey Bogart."

"I saw the film and I know who you're talking about. How often do they come in?" Lom asked.

"At least once a week. Sometimes more."

"Good. These are the guys who got in trouble about two years ago selling passports and driver's licenses. Right?"

"Yeah, you surely are. But they don't handle 'em anymore, at least that's what they told me. And after all the money they made on the dagger, you'd think they'd stay away from crap like that. Do you think there's a possibility they'll do passports for us?"

"Don't kid yourself. Those kinds of people always have blank ones left over, hidden away for a time when they can get rid of 'em safely. Well, they can give 'em to me and never get in trouble over it, and not getting in trouble with the law is their genuine concern right now. So, when they come in, tell 'em you have credit cards you want to trade for two passports for me and Toby. Here, take the two passports we took. Maybe they can change the picture somehow and we can use them and save those guys a lot of trouble. We'll need to take passport pictures, but that's easy. We can use your iPhone, take a few close-ups, and you can crop 'em and print 'em out. Why don't we do that now?"

Charlie obliged. Gosh, technology these days was great. You never even had to leave the comfort of your home to have a picture taken and printed. It was all so seamless.

Lom continued with his directions regarding the passports and credit cards. "Whatever way is the easiest and safest for those guys is the best way to go. You'll have to keep me posted on what they have to say about all of this. If they could use these passports, we'll still give them the credit cards as good faith. We'll keep the cash the dead men had in their wallets, and that'll be our traveling money."

"Damn, Lom, do you ever shut up? Do you enjoy hearing yourself talk?" a frustrated Charlie said.

"Did you count the cash out yet, Toby?" Lom asked, ignoring Charlie's comments.

"Not yet. I just stacked it on the table."

Lom looked at the pile of dough sitting on the table and said, "Well, step aside, Toby. Might as well count it now."

Toby had stacked the money into denominations — singles, five, tens, twenties, and so on. Lom sat down at the table. After he had finished counting, he looked up and said, "Your brother must have paid them well, Toby. There's over six thousand dollars here. That's enough to pay our expenses to your country.

Charlie, take one of the credit cards and buy two round-trip tickets to Talvania under one name on the credit card. Keep the credit card holder's license handy in case you're asked questions. Toby probably won't need a return ticket, but what the hell? We're not paying for them. Buy the tickets tonight, Charlie. You want to have it done before your passport guys come in?"

Charlie just shook his head. "Toby, don't be letting him order you around too much. You're a king." He laughed. "But it really doesn't matter to this ole fart. He could not care less. He orders around everybody. Okay, Lom, I'm outta here. Talk to you later."

After Charlie had left, Lom instructed Toby to remain in the room and not venture out. "I'm going to visit Martha and see how she's doing." Toby looked a little confused.

"Lom, Charlie is closed for the night. How are you going to get out of here if you can't go up the ladder and exit through the pawnshop?"

"There's another exit way up the line. You have to know where to find it because it's easy to miss. I'll use that exit and come back the same way."

That evening, at ten minutes before eleven, Lom once again entered the Good Burger diner and slid into his favorite booth. He knew her schedule like the back of his hand. Martha was busy in the back with a customer's order.

The swinging door of the kitchen opened, and Martha backed out, balancing a large tray of food. She walked past Lom and placed the platter of food on the table in front of the customers two booths down from Lom. Martha spotted him as soon as she turned to walk back to the kitchen. She walked toward his table. "Lom, what in hell are you doing here? What don't you get? Are you out of your cotton-pickin' mind? There must be a hundred men out there looking for you! Why in the hell do you keep coming back to one of the only two places they know they might find you?"

"Well, some would say I'm a mite off in my head, but so what? I live my life the way I want and if someone wants to make something of it, so be it," Lom said as he smiled.

Martha gazed at him sadly. "Lom, don't you understand you are no longer a young man? Look at yourself. You're getting older by the minute. How old are you, Lom? Seventy-five? Seventy-six? How old? Tell me."

Lom chuckled at seeing her frustration and her concern. "Hey, hey. You're way off, Martha. I'm only seventy-two years old, not seventy-six."

Martha smiled a sad smile. "Seventy-two or seventy-six. What's the difference? When are you going to realize it? You're no match for these guys. You killed four of their men. They're gonna kill you, Lom. Are you suicidal? Is that what you want—go down in a hail of bullets, some kind of hero?"

"Well, Martha, it looks like you're wrong again," he mused.

"What, you're not suicidal? Then you need to be committed. You are certifiably crazy!" she said, catching herself as she raised her voice.

"No, that's not it. You're wrong about me killing four men."

"You mean you didn't do it, Lom? Really? Then who did? I saw you, Lom. Are you going to start lying to me now? Don't start makin' me think I'm the crazy one, you ole goat!"

"It wasn't four men I killed. It's eight. You'll probably be hearing about those soon," he chuckled.

"What? You're telling me you killed eight of them?" And with that, she took the wipe up napkin she was using for her dirty tables and smacked him over the head with it.

"Well, no, not exactly. I only killed seven of them and Toby killed the other one. And a good thing he did because he was about to be kill me in about another second. But Toby took care of it. You know something? Come to think of it, you might be right. I plumb forgot about those two guys we shot outside the building, but… well… neither of us stopped to see if they was dead, but they probably was."

"Lom, in two skinny seconds, someone is going to see you– someone from the kitchen, someone working for these guys. Do yourself a favor. Disappear, go to Florida, go somewhere, anywhere where these men can't find you. Please, Lom. If you don't want to do it for yourself, then do it for me." There was dead silence.

Lom smiled that lopsided smile of his and put the two fingers of his right hand together as if he were pinching them. "Why, Martha, if I didn't know better," he said, "I'd think that you cared just a leeeettle bit for ole Lom here." He winked at her.

"Men!" Martha said, grabbing her cloth and throwing up her hands. She shook her head, turned away from him as if she had nothing more to say, and walked off, shaking her head, muttering words under her breath that sounded strangely like "bullheaded" or "thickheaded" or something to that effect, but he couldn't be sure.

Chapter Six

"What do you mean, they're all dead? They were the best of the best. These guys were mercenaries! All highly skilled mercenaries! They all fought in some of the most remote areas in the world and somebody killed them all?"

"It looks that way, boss."

"Who could be that good to take out eight of the best mercenaries money can buy? How many men do we have in the street right now?"

Chet didn't enjoy talking when he was this angry, but he said, "We have fifteen of our own men looking for the kid, and I called in a favor from the Russians. They sent ten additional men to join us on the hunt. I placed a reward–ten grand–for the guy who kills the kid."

"I don't like the idea of you going over my head to make a deal without my approval, but in this case, I'm glad that you did," the boss said as he tried to act upset.

Chet visibly relaxed. "What now, boss? What's our next move?"

"You know what? Let's raise that reward. Twenty-five grand for the guy who kills him in the next three days! That should add a little incentive to the party! You know these guys must want this kid dead in a hurry. They paid me two million to take care of it." Chet was stunned but tried not to look it. Kurt had taken Chet and two other men with him to Talvania, but Chet wasn't in the room when Kurt and Becker had made the deal. He didn't know how they structured the contract, and he certainly did not know the amount they had paid him.

Kurt continued, "Yeah, two million up front and another two million when we prove the kid's dead."

"Jesus, Kurt. Four million dollars was the bounty they placed on that kid's head? That's a hell of a lot of money for a hit," Chet chimed in.

"You're absolutely right, Chet, and that is exactly why we have to find this kid. He has to be somewhere in the city. He has to be real close, so why can't we find him? What about that pawnshop guy who said he had a lead on him? Did you pay him another visit?"

"No, not yet. He asked me to give him twenty-four hours, and he'd have something for me."

"Twenty-four hours, eh?"

"Yeah, twenty-four hours. Twelve hours are already on the clock."

"Good," Kurt said as he looked at his gold Rolex. "It's ten in the evening, so twelve hours from now would be ten tomorrow morning. You make sure you get there on time." Chet was about to leave, but Kurt stopped him. "Chet, what was the pawnbroker's story?"

"He has a hard-on for the old man because he stiffed him three months' rent. He only asked that if we find him I give him the rent money back. But I have no intention of doing that." Chet smirked.

"Okay, I've raised the reward from ten to twenty-five thousand and all this guy wants is his three months' rent and he's satisfied? Do the math. Why on earth would you chance an entire mission over such piddling little money? I don't want you to hurt him–I want this guy happy–so if giving him his rent money makes him happy, then I'm happy," Kurt said. "So what you'll do is see him at ten in the morning. Find out what he knows and if he has anything solid, then give him half his money up front and tell him you'll pay him the rest when we get the kid or the old man. Keep me posted on your every move."

"Done," Chet replied.

"Good! Talk to me tomorrow after you see this guy."

"You got it, boss." Chet left the room, relieved to be out of there. He was aware of Kurt's temper and he didn't want his wrath turned on him. The man was capable of anything, including killing his own men.

Chapter Seven

Lom was deep in thought as the two men braved the frosty night, walking from their hideout to board a train at the Forty-Second Street station. He was thinking of what Martha had said to him when he visited her at the restaurant and wondered what it all meant. Was concern for him like the concern of a daughter to a father? Or was she concerned because she might have feelings for him? He shrugged it off, telling himself that he was probably making too much of it, that he was too old for a gal like Martha. No matter; it was a nice feeling thinking that a pretty young woman like Martha might have feelings for him. How nice it would be to come home to an attractive woman. He thought he was beyond all that. Oh, how many years it had been since he had lain with a woman. He had given up on those stirrings, but now, here it was again, unexpectedly and refreshing. Funny, he thought, the heart is the same at any age.

Lom's time in Korea had limited his contact and time with the opposite sex. Thirty-five years in the army didn't allow for many opportunities to socialize with women, much less a quality woman. The army guys had their fill of prostitutes, rented them by the hour, and Lom, like the rest, readily seized those moments. As he had aged, his sex life had gradually slowed until it hit nonexistent. But now here was Martha, a breath of fresh air–a hard-working single mom raising two kids alone. The thought of being intimate with Martha brought back urges he'd long suppressed. He made himself a promise–if he made it through this mess, he would talk with Martha and see exactly what her feelings were, and he wouldn't hold it against her if she told him she only thought of him as a good friend. Then his mind went from curiosity to way off into the stratosphere. He wondered if she'd consider being his wife. He wondered if she was free to be anyone's wife. She did mention that they threatened to harm her family. He made a note to ask her exactly what she meant by that. Hell, he thought, I probably can't even perform at my age, but that, and many other thoughts, lingered as he and Toby exited the train and headed to the place on the paper that Charlie had given him. Thoughts of the future raced through his mind as they walked toward an address that might not allow him to return to Martha.

"Here we are," Toby said. "This is the address. How do you want to handle it? I don't see a guard."

"Neither do I," Lom responded, said to have his daydreams interrupted. "He must feel pretty safe. Thinks we don't know this address, so he didn't post a guard. That's a mistake on his part–a real amateurish move, if I say so myself. Look here, Toby, I want you to be my backup like you did when that guy tried to shoot me. But before we do anything, let's look at the perimeter. You check that side real quiet like and I'll check this side. I'll meet you at the rear of the building."

Lom trudged along the side of the two-story brick warehouse. There was nothing unusual to set off any alarms. When he reached the rear of the building, Toby was in the shadows, waiting for him near the back door. "Pssst... over here, Lom." Lom walked over to where Toby was hiding.

"Did you see anybody?" Toby asked.

"No. Check the back door," Lom whispered. There was a large loading platform with a wide overhead door that swung up either remotely or by hand, but they were more interested in the door beside it.

"They wouldn't leave it open, but check it anyway," Lom said.

Toby glided over, tugged on the door, but they locked it. It was an old door with an old lock and, more important, it didn't have a padlock on it.

"Give me your knife," Toby whispered. Lom quickly obliged and handed him the big Randall. Carefully, Toby pressed the blade between the tang and the jam and gently pulled the door open toward him.

"Pretty impressive, Toby," Lom whispered. "Now let's be real quiet going in." Once inside, both men walked silently up the loading ramp leading in from the back door. There was a staircase on the left and a large, vacant, concrete floor room with a few boxes in the rear on their right. They checked the receiving room. It was empty. An unlit, half-smoked cigar rested in an ashtray on a small table beside a reclining chair, all facing a television set. They backtracked to the staircase. Lom was holding the silenced PPKS. Not trusting his hearing, Lom whispered to Toby, "Do you hear anything?"

"No. Nothing."

"Then let's check upstairs," Lom said, motioning the gun in that direction.

The two men began their ascent, not knowing if the stairs would creak or groan. The stairs cooperated and the two men made it all the way to the top without making a sound. They walked down the hall, checking the rooms on either side of them as they passed. There was an empty room on Toby's left and one on the right of Lom. The last room was an office. There was no one there. Lom, half disappointed, found a pad from the desk, ripped off a page, plucked a pen from its holder, and wrote a note to the resident of the warehouse: "I HEARD YOU WERE LOOKING FOR ME. NOW I'M LOOKING FOR YOU!" He signed it: THE OLD MAN. Lom placed the note in the middle of the pad on the desk, and turned to Toby, motioning for him to back out of the warehouse.

They exited the same way they had entered — through the back door. When they neared the neighborhood, instead of going back to their hideout, Lom reconsidered and paid Martha a quick visit. Outside the Good Burger, Lom asked Toby to hide in the same place he used when the men were looking for him.

"I need to talk to Martha for a few minutes and I sure would appreciate you watching out for me," Lom said. "If any of those wise guys pull up, keep your eyes on what they do. Follow them in the restaurant if they come in. If they stay outside, then you stay hidden and watch 'em. I won't be more than a few minutes, and then we'll hightail it out of here."

Lom walked through the door, surprising Martha yet once again. Here he was, like old times, with that crooked smile of his. "Hi, Martha."

"Lom, I cannot believe you came back!" Martha huffed. "Now tell me WHAT EXACTLY are you doing here, AGAIN?"

"I came here to ask you a few questions, Martha, and after I get my answer, I'll be on my way."

"And what questions, Lom, could be so all-fire important that you took another ridiculous chance of getting yourself killed? What could you possibly want to ask me?"

"When you said that you had family to worry about, what family would that be, Martha?" Lom asked directly.

"My two children and my mother. That's the family I was talking about. Why? What?? That's what you came here to ask me?" she said as she looked around, checking the kitchen door.

"No husband, Martha?"

"No, we divorced eight years ago, and he took up with another woman. He died in an accident two years ago."

"Do you have any feelings for me, Martha?" he asked, just running from one question into another, throwing Martha completely off guard. She was speechless for what seemed an eternity. Her mouth moved, but no words came out.

Flustered, she finally said, "Well, of course, I have feelings for you."

"Martha, I don't mean feelings like you have for your father or your brother. I mean, do you have actual feelings for me?"

"Oh, please, Lom," she said dismissively. "This is not the time for such foolishness!"

"Please don't say it like that, Martha. This is not foolishness that I'm talking about. I'm dead earnest. Please don't make fun."

"Lom, Lom, I'm not making fun of it. It's just that I don't think this is the time for such talk," she said, still glancing around the room.

"Well, I think you're wrong there, Martha," Lom continued. "This may be the only time I'll be able to ask you that question. Now, look right in my face and tell me yes or no. It's that simple. Yes or... no?"

Martha's head tilted down as she twisted her hands nervously in her lap. Once again, the silence was deafening. Her mind was racing and her heart was having a hard time keeping up with it.

"All right, Lom," she said sternly. "You asked me a question and I guess you're entitled to an answer, so here it is. Yes, I have feelings for you and I have had feelings for you for seven years now. I always thought you'd think that the difference in our ages would be a problem and that it might prevent any kind of... WHATEVER between us."

Lom tried to contain his words and simply smiled. "Well, you're right, Martha," he agreed. "My age might have been a game changer before the shootout in here, but since then, I've had a lot of time to think and I gotta tell you I've always thought you're a real nice person and one fine-looking woman. All this craziness has made me think a little bit about things, questions that I have. Now that you've answered them, I just want you to know that you've made me feel alive again. I can't wait for all this nonsense to be over."

Martha looked towards the door. "Lom, where's Toby? Is he in your hideout?"

"He's outside, watching my back. I told him I would only be a few minutes, so I guess I'd better be getting on my way. But when this is all finished, you and me will take a little vacation. How's that sound?"

"It sounds great," she smiled and said. "Now don't you go getting yourself killed on me. You take care of yourself. I don't want to lose you now that we've cleared the air a bit. Not that I ever wanted to. Oh, you have me so flustered I can't even talk. Go! Get outta here!"

"Don't you worry none about that," Lom said. "I'll be back. You wait and see." And with that, he smiled and marched straight toward the door. If he'd been younger, hell, he thought, he might have skipped all the way out, but this old soldier had to keep some decorum about him.

Chapter Eight

Martha left work in the evening feeling a little light-headed. She never expected her life to take a turn like this. Years ago, Martha's husband had asked for a divorce. As soon as they completed it, he had taken off with another woman. Essentially, Martha had raised two children all by herself, working nights, so she could be with them when they needed her. She did a fine job of it, too. For years, she had worked long hours, juggling two jobs. The reward was that her son had finished college with honors and had gone on to law school. After passing the bar, he went to work for Haynes and Nash, a small law firm in Maryland. Over ten years, the firm had grown and prospered. Last year, he called his mother to give her the good news–he had just made partner. Tom always acknowledged his mother's hard work and the sacrifices she made for him, and always vowed to make it up to her. From the time he drew his first small salary, he had always sent something to his mother, who still struggled to give his sister the same education she had given him. He was a good boy, a kind, appreciative son.

Martha's daughter, Olivia, eventually was accepted to NYU. During her first year in college, she met a young medical student. It didn't take long before the relationship was serious. While engaged to be married, Olivia quit school and found a job so she could help support her soon-to-be husband in his career. She found a job working for a local lawyer. Olivia was one of those intuitive employees, always expecting what her bosses might need and having it on their desks before they asked. Whether it was a brief, a file, or their calendar for the week, she had it ready for them. The attorneys depended on her. It wasn't long before they promoted her to office manager. Because of her organizational ability, the lawyers discovered they had more time to devote to their clients and more free time for themselves. Olivia was all about efficiency, studying each client's files. It was then that she discovered wasted hours; some because of poor work ethics, some because of little reliance on a computer. It was simply the way the firm had done business since Day One. Olivia spent much of her free time reviewing procedures. Billable hours were being lost to research, so thus began her challenge. She broke down each of the existing cases and spread the work out evenly, assigning the research to the firm's legal assistants, freeing the attorneys to concentrate on trial preparation. She became indispensable, and the law firm of Coogan, Miles, and Farbstein duly noted it. A series of pay increases ensued until Olivia earned enough to help her fiancé through medical school without occurring student loans. The couple lived with Martha, and Olivia contributed to the rent, electricity, and all the household necessities. Martha's days of worrisome provision for her family were nearing an end.

One sunny, spring day in June, Tom, Olivia's brother and Martha's son, walked his sister down the aisle to be wed to her soon to be husband, Dr. Daniel Foster. They remained happily married to this day.

Martha hadn't thought about romance since her husband had left her. Her two children were her focus. Now that the kids were gone, things were different. Her kids had been such a large part of her life, and taking care of them had required almost all of her time and attention. One day she was working nights, struggling to raise her kids, and now she was all alone. It happened fast. It had paid off with two successful children, but now empty nest syndrome had set in and reality came with it.

Martha was in her fifties with no kids and no man, but she had a job she enjoyed. Her interaction with her regular customers was a big part of her enjoyment. When she went to work in the evenings, it was like visiting with relatives, especially Lom. She always got a kick out of him. He was worldly in his own folksy way. He always treated her so nicely. She knew he lived alone and that he had only one friend, Charlie, who owned the pawnshop down the street. Lom never had a bad day, always entered the restaurant with a smile. He always had a pleasant word for her and he normally kidded her about something. Martha would play along and keep the banter going. Over the years, she looked forward to seeing him. On her days off, she thought about him and that crooked smile. For an old man, he stood straight, had all of his hair, and it wasn't even completely white. It was a pleasant shade of gray that she knew eventually would fade to white. He wasn't a bad-looking man, either. It was just that he had lost his youthful good looks. She could tell that he must have been really handsome when he was young.

Martha would always ask Lom to bring in some photos of him in his youth. He questioned why she wanted to see those pictures of him. Curiosity, he guessed. Martha was still was an attractive woman and worldly in how a woman who worked nights in a restaurant could be. Over the years, she had met many men. She could pick out the hustlers, the wise guys, and the good ones, and there was something special about Lom. She had even fantasized about what life would be like married to Lom. Her mind would then turn to hard reality like... how many years would she have with him? There was this big age difference, after all.

That Lom. He was full of surprises. A few short hours ago, he shocked her by walking into the restaurant and asking her straight out if she had any feelings for him. Martha recounted her loss for words and how silly she felt. That question was something she had dreamed about for several years and when he confronted her, she acted like a little schoolgirl. He could have left the restaurant that day, thinking she didn't care for him. Oh, how happy she was that she spilled the beans. They had rather agreed on something, but what it was, she wasn't sure, but the thought was really warm and promising. He had said something about a vacation, that much she knew, and that brought a smile to her face. She would really love to go on a trip with him. A vacation was something she had deprived herself of while raising her kids. Now that they were gone, she could think of herself a little—a vacation with her secret crush might be just the thing to allow her to live again. She would go wherever Lom took her.

At the moment of these pleasantries, reality set in. It was if a dark shadow passed over her. What if he doesn't come back? She thought. What if those men kill him? What would I do then? I just found the man I want to be with and I wouldn't know how to handle it if they killed him. This was like one of those tear-jerking war stories. No, I can't think of that now, she said to herself, shaking off those thoughts. I don't want to send him negative thoughts. Once again, she pictured them on vacation, on a little beach somewhere, and she fantasized about the mystical places where he might take her. Then she thought about sleeping with him. What would that be like? Martha felt herself becoming aroused. Better I send him these thoughts, she chuckled to no one, than the ones I was dwelling on before.

Chapter Nine

"Charlie, pick up. It's Lom."

"I'm here. What's happening?"

"Listen, Charlie, we went to visit the second address you gave us. It's a warehouse, but no one was there,, so I left the man a note instead, telling him I was now looking for HIM. I figured I'd give him a little something to think about. Now listen to me. These boys are most likely furious at my little visit last night, so they're probably gonna visit you early this morning wanting information about me. You gotta tell them you have good news. Tell them that in three days, you'll have an address on me. Tell them I won't be there until three days from now. If they ask you for the address now, tell them you don't have it, but it's coming, and you'll have it real soon. Tell them you told an informer that you'd give him that ole antique chest that's been sitting there, you know the one you paid twenty-five dollars for, and tell 'em that he said he'd deliver the information. They might ask you who it was, so you tell them it was a friend of a customer who comes in once in a while. Make up some excuse why you can't give his name away. You're a smart guy, even though you try hard not to show it. Understand what I'm telling you to say? Now if you have questions, ask them now."

"No, I don't have any fool questions for you," Charlie snarled. "What do you think? I'm a moron? And you better be careful how you answer."

Lom smiled. He knew Charlie would take the bait.

Promptly at ten o'clock in the morning, the bell on the door sprang to life, alerting Charlie that he had visitors. The brawny man with the mad face approached the counter where Charlie was busy tinkering with one of his newly owned pawned items.

"Hi there, Chet."

Chet didn't bother with pleasantries. He got right to the point. "I hope for your sake you have something for me."

"Well, I do, and then again, I don't."

Before Charlie could say another word, Chet grabbed him by his collar and yanked his face close to his. "Don't play games with me, little man. I want to know what you found out. And it better be good." Chet felt something hard against his stomach, and he looked down to see an automatic pressed against his gut.

"I'd appreciate it if you'd give me a little room to catch my breath, Chet. I wouldn't want this gun here with the hair trigger to go off accidental like." Chet glared for a half second and released the collar. He backed away slowly, and Charlie lowered the gun to his side.

"That's more like it. Now, do you want to hear my news?" Charlie asked. "Which do you want first–the good news or the bad news?"

"Look, just tell me what you know and I'll decide what's good and what's bad. Now talk!" Chet said, raising his voice.

"I'll give you the good news first. I'll have the location of the place where the guy's staying, and that's a fact. The bad news is–he won't be there for another three days. I guess he's moving around a lot, trying hard to stay away from you guys. But this information is costing me more than I was figuring on. I had to promise this ole chest here that's worth about two thousand dollars, so add that to the three-months' rent I lost and you're talking about some serious money. At least to me it's serious, cause I'm out of pocket for twenty-three hundred dollars."

Charlie explained how he'd visited a dozen of the old man's hangouts and had asked many people if they knew where the old man was. "As it would happen, the guy who knew walked right into his store. This guy was down on his luck, friend of a customer who comes in occasionally, and wouldn't tell me anything unless I paid him something up front. He told me he wanted a grand now and another thousand in three days. I knew he'd been eyeing this chest for his house or his mother, or whatever, so I made him a deal. The chest is worth two grand. I didn't pay that for it, of course, but that's its value. That's when he said he would know for sure where the old man would be. I agreed to give him the chest the minute he has somethin' that pans out. He also told me the kid was with him."

Chet's eyes grew wide, hearing that the kid was still with the old man. This was good news. Chet visibly relaxed.

Charlie continued. "My contact said the old man was protecting him sort of like a father would. He told me that the old man doesn't trust anybody and that's why he keeps moving round a lot. Told me not to worry about finding him, just give him half of what's due now. I gave him some old coins that he has to return to get the chest. Said he'd be back in three days. I told you I'd find out where he is. You boys been looking for him for a good while now and couldn't find him, but I found him in just a few days. Now just back off a bit, give me a little time, and I'll give you the old man. But remember–I want my twenty-three hundred dollars in cash when I hand over his address. Now we had a deal, and I kept my end of the bargain. I would expect you to do the same and keep yours."

"And just what makes you think this guy is telling the truth?" Chet barked.

"I know a man who's lying and who's tellin' the truth. This guy's telling the truth, and besides, I know how to find him if he screws me."

Chet didn't know what to make of this information. He did not relish the thought of going back to Kurt to tell him he wouldn't have the address for another three days. He thought about the kid and he relaxed. Chet had no choice. Now that he knew the kid was with the old man, he could put a positive spin on the story. After all, it wasn't like he had made no progress. He'd gotten farther than any of the others. He now had what appeared to be a positive lead. So what if he had to wait three days for the address? Chet felt certain that the little man standing in front of him knew what might happen if he didn't deliver in the three days. Chet liked that thought and smiled for only the second time since this nightmare began. With the kid still in the picture, this was a good thing.

Chapter Ten

The cell phone rang, and Kurt quickly answered. "I'm here. What do you have for me?"

"I have some pretty good news," Chet said. "See you in twenty minutes." Kurt was eager to hear it, right now, but he knew the dangers of phone conversations. He placed the cell phone on his desk and tapped his fingers, nervously awaiting Chet's return.

The coast was clear. Charlie picked up his radio and clicked twice. Lom answered immediately.

"Okay, Charlie, what happened?"

"Well," Charlie explained, "they came in at exactly ten o'clock this morning like they said they would, and I told that big guy with the mean face–Chet–what you told me to tell him." Charlie laid it all out for Lom, telling him everything that was said from the time they arrived to the time they left. "And you know, Lom, I had some uneasy moments with these guys. The one called Chet had me by my throat until I put a gun in his ribs and mentioned that the kid was still with you. That changed everything. The kid is the one they're after, but they want you, too, for killing their men, and I'm assuming you must have pissed them off over the note you left them."

"Charlie," Lom said, ignoring his last comment. "Let's get back to Chet for a minute. Tell me exactly how he reacted when you told him the kid was still with me."

"There was a big change in his attitude. He seemed to lighten up a bit. I even thought I saw a faint glimmer of a smile cross his face when I mentioned the kid. I figure they might have thought the kid had somehow got away, maybe left the state, but he sure seemed relieved hearing that the kid was still here. What ya think?"

"They must have paid Chet's boss must a lot of money to kill Toby here, and when the plan didn't go the way they figured, then it got a little complicated. The kid got away and now there's a lot of pressure on Chet's boss 'cause he has to find the kid and kill him in order to fulfill his end of the bargain. So hearing that the kid was still in town takes a lot of the pressure off of Chet. Now he can go back to his boss and give him some good news for a change. Here I am talking to you as if no one could listen in on our conversation. You know where I am, so I'd appreciate it if you could bring us a bite to eat. We're getting pretty hungry."

"Will do. See you in an about an hour," Charlie said.

"Thanks. See you in an hour," Lom echoed. And both men signed off.

Approximately ten minutes later, Charlie locked the door to his pawnshop and walked the short block to the local KFC. The weather was a chilly forty degrees and Charlie walked briskly, thinking that this was the longest one block he'd ever walked. Inside, he ordered a large box of original recipe, three orders of biscuits, two orders of their famous mashed potatoes and gravy, and some green beans. He paid and walked back to his store, and re-entered the warmth of his shop.

Outside, Chet's men stood shivering. Both men had watched as Charlie left and returned, carrying the bag of Kentucky Fried Chicken. One man placed a call.

"Chet, the guy left and bought some things at KFC. He's back now, inside, with the food. It looks to me like they won't be going anywhere. It's too cold to go anywhere. The weather is almost unbearable out here. What do you want us to do?"

"Yes, you're probably right," Chet said. "He's probably in for the night. I'm pulling you in. Head over to the warehouse," he said. It made no sense to leave his men there in the freezing cold.

No one inside the Brooklyn warehouse heard as the back door opened. The intruders hugged the wall, trying to make themselves as small as possible. They held their guns high and walked stealthily toward the sound of voices. It was as if the two men were replaying their visit to the Hudson Street warehouse a few nights ago. If only they could be as lucky here as they were before. They walked along a five-foot wide path– the corridor that allowed employees to walk freely when they packed the warehouse with freight containers full of merchandise waiting to be shipped.

"I'm going to walk in and have me a little talk with these fellas. You stay in the shadows. Try not to make a sound. Cover me."

Lom was glad he had convinced Charlie that he shouldn't come along with them. It was bad enough worrying about himself and Toby. It would have been much different with a third person, especially his good friend Charlie.

Lom also understood the difference between the risks. Fifty years ago, he was a match for anyone his age, but now Lom knew that if anyone knocked him down at this age, he'd be lucky to get back on his feet in time to defend himself. Charlie was right. Using a gun was one thing, but reflexes were another. He sure wasn't planning on using his fists to fight these younger guys. Lom still couldn't figure out why the one thing left intact, beside his aim, was his sight. Why the good Lord allowed him to maintain his wonderful vision was an anomaly. What old man had such vision? So, he had his sight, and he had his gun. And as long as he had a gun, no one on earth was more deadly–

young or old. Lom's marksmanship was something in which he had complete confidence.

Lom checked his nineteen eleven Colt automatic to make sure he had a full magazine. He pulled back the receiver to insert a round into the chamber. Satisfied, he placed the big automatic back into his shoulder holster and continued with the same procedure for the silenced little Walther PPKS. The Walther had a suppressor on it and he knew that up close; he didn't need the stopping power of the forty-five. At close range, the little PPKS could be as deadly as an automatic.

Lom held the Walther at his side and walked quietly toward a room in the building's front where he heard voices. Toby positioned himself in a recessed doorway and observed. It was obvious to Lom that this was the main office, the one used to conduct the business that took place here. The office had large glass windows with a five-foot wooden section below it. He figured it allowed the boss to monitor things, to see who was working, who wasn't, and the progress of the freight. From his vantage point, he could see three men. Lom needed to get to the other side of the room to scope out the rest of the office, to see if there were other occupants. He made a quick decision to crawl the length of the five-foot section of wall. By staying close to the wall, he figured he would pass unnoticed. He was taking a big chance. If someone exited the office, it would be difficult for Lom to go from his horizontal position to standing in a matter of seconds. He continued along past the windows, inching quietly and slowly toward the other side.

Just feet away, he heard a noise behind him. The man never saw Lom... until it was too late. It happened quickly. Lom, flat on his back, raised his gun hand, extended it over his head, and fired. The man went down. Being on his back had given Lom full advantage. He could hear the man seconds before being seen.

Toby, meanwhile, had observed the man approaching Lom. He had tried to get Lom's attention by waving his hand and calling out in a soft voice. Toby wondered what the old man was up to when he put his hand over his head. And that was when he saw him shoot. The gunshot had hit the man in the larger mass area of the chest and the man had tumbled to the ground, barely making a sound. The men inside the office didn't hear the tiny cough of the silenced gunshot. Lom and Toby had been lucky with this one. The warehouse men saw nothing, heard nothing. Lom struggled to his feet. The effort caused him to breathe hard for a few seconds. He took a moment to collect himself, looked toward Toby's hideout, and glimpsed him. Content that his backup was still in place, Lom boldly walked to the office door, threw it open, and yelled, "Keep your hands where I can see them."

"Who the hell are you?" one man yelled.

"Now where's your manners, young fella?" Lom asked calmly. He was in his element. Lom seemed unshakable. "I'm the one holding the gun, so I'm supposed to be the one who's asking the questions. Now, what I want each of you to do is to reach deep into your fancy jacket pockets and take your guns out real nice and easy like, and lay them on that table over there, real slow, one at a time, where I can see. Come on now. I know that you have them, so take 'em out. Put them on the table."

The men first looked at each other. Lom cocked the gun and with that, one man yelled, "Hold on. I'm doing it. Gimme a second." One by one, the other men followed suit, some slowly reaching inside their jackets, others down toward their ankles. Each systematically placed a gun on the table, except for the man on the left. Suddenly, he reached for his gun and aimed it toward Lom. As fast as lightning, Lom whirled around and shot him. The man fell off his chair and clanked to the floor. Lom just stood there, shaking his head. The room fell silent as the men all sat stunned at what they'd just witnessed. This old man was serious.

"Easy now," Lom said, as if speaking to a group of children. "Don't get any funny ideas. This gun I'm holding has a hair trigger and sometimes, just sometimes, it goes off for no reason at all. Sheeeiit," he continued. "You see what I'm telling you? This gun almost has a mind of its own, shooting your friend like that. I sure didn't mean to kill him, but it's this damn gun here, and besides, he was planning on doing me some harm and I just can't let anything like that happen, right? Now, why don't we all get to talking?" he said as he pulled up a chair and seated himself, his gun still trained on the men. "I'd like to know why everyone is looking for me. I sure as hell did nothing to you boys. Will somebody please answer my question?"

The room was silent still. Lom's eyes scanned the room. He looked first at one man, then another, and randomly pointed his gun at one of them, then at another and another. "Anyone? Come on now. I've been real nice to you boys, but if you don't start answering my questions, why, I'm just going to kill you all, one at a time. If you don't talk, then you're of no use to me at all."

One guy looked at Lom and sneered, "Go fuck yourself, old man." Lom calmly raised his gun and shot the man right through the heart.

"Two down and two to go," Lom said matter-of-factly. "Actually, it's really three down, counting the one outside the room here."

There were two remaining men, both visibly shaken by what they'd seen. One had turned a pasty white and the other's eyes had expanded to the size of golf balls. They looked at each other, almost seeking approval.

"Okay, okay, enough shooting. We'll talk."

"I'm only gonna say this once," Lom responded, "so you better be paying attention. If I feel you're lying to me, I'm gonna kill you without another word said. Tell me the truth–you live. You have my word on that. Are we agreed now that you know the rules?"

The two men nodded in agreement.

"Good! Now tell me why you fellas are looking to kill me?"

"It's not you we want," the younger of the two answered. "It's the kid that my boss wants. If you give him to us, all will be great. We go on our way and everything is nice and peaceful."

"Well, that's rather kind of you, fellas. You're gonna let ME go. Well, that's a real comfort. But I have a problem with that. I killed ten of your men, and I don't think your boss will just let me walk away. I don't know if I could just let me walk away if I was your boss. Does that make any sense to you?"

The men nodded again. They knew Lom was right. Kurt would never, could never, let him live now.

Lom smiled at the men. "You catch my drift, fellas? He's never going to stop till he kills me. But you want to know something?" He pointed his gun at them, suggesting they answer and answer quickly.

"Yes," the men responded in unison.

"You see." Lom continued. "I've killed over three hundred fifty men in my life and I'm sure as hell not afraid of anybody in this room or, for that matter, anywhere. Now I'd appreciate it if one of you would tell me who your boss is and where I can find him." Lom looked at one, then at the other, and pointed his gun toward the larger of the two men and said, "You! What's your boss's name and where do I find him?"

The man hesitated. "I will not ask you again," Lom said sternly. "I know that you're afraid of what your boss will do to you when he finds out that you gave me information. Now nod your head if I'm right." Both men nodded almost at the same time. "Good. Now here's what's about to happen. You see, your boss is a pussy because, right now, I'm the one you have to fear. You know why?"

This time, they bobbed their heads nervously.

"The reason you should be afraid of ME rather than HIM is because I'm the one holding the barrel that you're staring at and I'll kill both of you, just like I did those other two fellas over there." Lom raised his gun and pointed it at the big man's head. The man squinted and tried to recoil from the gun, but the gun he fixated on the center of his forehead.

"Wait. Don't kill me. I'll tell you anything you want to know, but don't kill me. Please."

"Well, that's more like it," Lom said sarcastically. "Now who is this guy and where do I find him?"

The men began talking quickly, stepping on each other's lines, until Lom was pleased that he had everything he needed. Lom raised his gun, which sent the two men cowering and begging. "Please, you promised us you wouldn't kill us. We talked. We answered your questions."

Lom shook his head. "Now don't you worry, fellas. I'm a man of my word. I'm not gonna kill you, I'm just gonna make sure that you're out of action for a little while. I don't want you boys doggin' me or the kid anymore." Lom shot both men in their knees.

Chapter Eleven

Ten o'clock in the morning was becoming an important time of the day for Charlie. Yesterday, it was Chet and his boys, and today, the bell tinkled for the passport guys. Victor, standing there smiling, reminded Charlie of Sydney Greenstreet in the Maltese Falcon. He looked as if he could have been his twin brother.

Charlie smiled as Victor walked in. This was unusual because most of the time, Charlie frowned when he came in. Something was up, and Victor knew it.

"Hi, boys. I'm real glad to see you."

"Yeah, why's that?" Victor said, amused. He knew Charlie wanted something.

"Because I have something I'd like to trade with you." That got Victor's attention.

"What do you have to trade? And what do you want in return?"

"I like a man who comes right to the point, Victor. Do you remember all the times you came in here asking for credit card information and I told you I'm not into that kind of stuff? Well, today, I have a few credit cards for you."

"Really? Huh. Why the sudden change of heart?"

"Well," Charlie said. "We did some business before and we both did pretty well with it. Thought I'd give it another go. This is a onetime deal, fellas. I like you boys when you don't talk credit card shit, but today is different. Today, I'm makin' an exception. I need two passports. I even have two passports to give you, if you can use them."

Charlie grabbed the passport photos of Lom and Toby that were lying on the cash register and passed the pictures and the two passports to Victor. Victor put on his reading glasses, looked at the passports, then at the pictures, and scrutinized them both in an almost professorial manner. He smiled and said, "These will do. I can use these."

"That's good," Charlie said. "Because my friends could use the credit cards that go with these names. These boys are no longer with the living, so they won't mind us using them. Makes it a lot easier, don't ya think? The other two credit cards are what I'm paying you with. This is to be a complete package. Fix the driver's licenses and the passports and we have a deal. The credit cards are good, but use 'em in a hurry."

"All right. Wonderful stuff. Having the photos and the licenses, it won't be hard to put the photos onto the passports. It'll look like when they issued the original passports, these photos were on them. When do you need them?"

"In a week?"

"That works out fine for me," Victor said.

Charlie had another thought. "Victor, I don't know if you can do this, but I'd like you to do me another favor."

Victor looked up. Charlie never talked much. This was the first time Victor could remember Charlie saying more than a few words in conversation. Victor enjoyed visiting with Charlie. He knew he could confide in him and, although Charlie might not approve of his "profession," he knew he wouldn't pass anything on to the authorities. Victor had a legitimate business, too, but he sometimes used it as a front for his at-times illegal side businesses. Hustle was in Victor's blood. He was like a druggie, unable to control himself when an opportunity to make money came his way.

Charlie occasionally would find Victor the odd or rare item he'd been searching for. Victor visited Charlie's pawnshop once or twice a week, looking for something unusual. Charlie's coup d'état was when he supplied Victor with a rare jeweled dagger from the twelfth century. No one else could find it. Charlie did, and that sale made both Victor and Charlie fairly wealthy men. That money went a long way to secure Charlie a nice retirement.

There was a story behind that dagger. A retired jewel thief bought some hard-to-find military gear from Charlie. Charlie knew the thief by his reputation. People in Charlie's business know each other, dealt with each other in the quest for certain items. It was common knowledge to the top, high-end thieves, but one thing everyone knew well was that Charlie wouldn't deal with stolen goods, no matter how tempting. Even the local police respected Charlie. They knew him to be a hard-working, honest businessman.

The jewel thief assured Charlie that he was now completely legitimate, stating that at present he was working for the government and even showed Charlie his government I.D. The ex-thief was an amiable fellow and whenever he visited the pawnshop, he always came with another man, a hard man that he introduced as Mickey.

Meanwhile, Victor had asked Charlie to do him a favor and be on the lookout for a twelfth century dagger, stating that he'd appreciate Charlie calling him right away should a seller come in. Victor claimed the dagger was for a wealthy client who collected rare medieval knives and daggers and was looking to add to his collection. When the ex-jewel thief came in looking at the unusual military gear Charlie carried, Charlie mentioned he was looking for a particular dagger. The jewel thief immediately stopped browsing and questioned Charlie about it. After hearing the details, the man surprised Charlie by telling him he could get it for him. Charlie clarified the dagger wasn't for him, but for one of his customers who had a client who wanted this piece and that money was no object, provided the dagger was legitimate. The thief emphatically stated that he could get it.

"Don't worry," the ex-thief said. "It's perfectly legitimate and the best example of its kind anywhere in the world. You can check it with stolen property records at the police station before you call your customer."

That satisfied Charlie for the moment. Charlie looked at the young man and said, "You know, mister, I don't even know your name."

"Lucky. Call me Lucky."

Barely a week later, Lucky returned, carrying the knife. Charlie knew the pawn business. Over the years, they had offered him well-made counterfeit items, but mostly, he never failed to spot the fake, no matter the item. This knife was different, very different. It was in like-new condition, which was confusing. How was that possible with a twelfth century dagger? Charlie removed his jeweler's loop and examined every aspect. He studied the gemstones set into the handle. They were real and of good quality; he was sure. The blade didn't have a scratch on it, was shiny like silver, and as sharp as a razor. The more he examined the dagger, the more its exquisite beauty took him. Satisfied that it was real, he grabbed his phone and called Victor, expressing a sense of urgency. When Victor arrived, Charlie introduced him to Lucky and showed him the knife. Victor's face was priceless. "Mother of God," he said as he kept examining the knife, twisting it, holding it to the light, turning it from every angle.

"This is exactly what my client is looking for. How do we work this out?" Victor asked while barely taking his eyes off the knife.

"Lucky?" Charlie asked.

"This knife is too rare to trust in anyone's care, so when you visit your buyer, I'll come along to protect my investment."

Lucky watched Charlie watching him and put his hands up in surrender. "Don't worry," Lucky said. "I'm not interested in going around you and stealing your customer. I just want my end of it–anywhere from twenty-five to fifty million for this knife and if your client buys it, you are both rich men. I'm already pretty well off financially, but I won't let this dagger out of my sight."

Lucky had certainly caught the attention of Victor and Charlie. Those were staggering numbers, and the amount made Victor suspicious. He was used to dealing with impressive numbers, but never this large. Victor looked at Lucky as if they were opponents in a poker game, studying him to see if he was bluffing. No matter how hard he stared, Victor couldn't read this young thief. Finally Victor said, "All right. How do you suggest we proceed?"

Lucky replied candidly, "It's simple. Like I said, I'll go along with you. I'll keep my mouth shut and let you do the negotiating. I suggest you pick up the phone now and call your client and tell him to have his appraiser with him when we visit him and while you have him on the phone, emphasize what he may already know–that this is a rare one-of-a-kind jeweled dagger unlike anything he is likely to have in his collection. If he's interested, it'll cost him millions. If he doesn't balk, we'll pay him a visit. Now, if he buys the knife, I will pay you ten percent of whatever price it sells for, and you and Charlie can split that. Do the math, gentlemen. Ten percent of fifty million is five million dollars, two point five million each. The more I get, the more you get. Do your best to make it happen. Agreed?"

Victor and Charlie both nodded, but there was still much work to do. Charlie contacted every resource he had, checking to see if it was a stolen dagger. Each time, it came back clean. Convinced that the item was legitimate, Victor finally made the call to set an appointment with Mr. Hugo Rothschild, but Rothschild, barely able to contain his excitement, insisted that the men come over immediately. Charlie phoned Lucky and asked if he could meet them in a half hour at the Rothschild address. Rothschild told Victor that he would notify building security of their visit.

Charlie and Victor couldn't help but wonder if this Mr. Rothschild was related to THE well-known Rothschild family. Lucky didn't care. This Mr. Rothschild lived on Park Avenue and Seventy-Eighth Street in the penthouse. When the three men arrived at Rothschild's hotel, security instantly recognized their names. After logging their names, a security man escorted them into the elevator and accompanied them to the penthouse. The elevator opened, and a housekeeper was waiting. She escorted the men into an expansive living room where Hugo Rothschild and another man were waiting. The three visitors surmised that the other man must be Rothschild's trusted appraiser, apparently on standby for occasions such as these.

With introductions and formalities completed, Victor gingerly placed the wooden dagger case onto the coffee table in front of them. He paused before opening it. "Mr. Rothschild, I'd love to see your collection of medieval daggers," he said in a questioning manner.

"Sure," Rothschild answered. "Follow me." Rothschild led the men into what must have been the third bedroom, but was now a small museum. "Oohs" and "wows" filled the room. The rare collection of medieval cutlery was impressive. He displayed each piece beautifully, with engraved plates detailing its uniqueness and history. Charlie couldn't help but notice that Lucky looked a little bored.

When they returned to the living room, Victor knelt before the case, and purposely, as if to tease the potential buyer, opened it in what seemed to be slow motion. Rothschild's eyes widened as the perfect specimen of a twelfth century dagger revealed itself. He reached in, picked it up, stared at it, turned it, and caressed it for quite some time. The Park Avenue collector was holding a dagger far superior to anything in his collection–a collection considered one of the most complete of its kind in the world. He held the dagger up to the light and examined its precious jewels, mesmerized by the cascade of colors reflecting off of the stones.

"I've been collecting these daggers for most of my adult life and nothing, but nothing, has ever come close to the beauty of the one I'm holding." He turned to his guest, the man already there when Charlie, Victor, and Lucky arrived, and handed him the knife. The appraiser took the dagger and studied it for a long time with his high-powered loupe, looking for any signs of a knock-off or fake, or for something that might scream authentic. The process seemed to last forever.

"Harry," Rothschild said. "Surely you must know something by now. You work for Christie's, for heaven's sakes!"

Unaffected by the comment, Harry the appraiser continued to study the piece, slowly and methodically examining every inch of the knife. At last, he looked up. A smile inched across his lips. "It's definitely real." Rothschild, until this point, had remained totally emotionless, but he let out an audible breath, signifying relief. He smiled back, eyes wide open, and stood speechless for a few seconds.

Billionaire Hugo Rothschild bought the ornately bejeweled twelfth century dagger for forty-two million dollars. They completed the deal right there. They wired the money into Lucky's account and he paid them their commissions on the spot. Charlie was curious and then asked the young man how he got possession of such a rare and treasured collectible. The young man shook his head and laughed, stating, "You wouldn't believe me if I told you."

"What's the favor you need, Charlie?" Victor asked.

"I need you to have two guns waiting for my friends when they arrive in Talvania. Can you arrange it?"

Victor, always the businessman, did a mental count of his customers who might accommodate him. He hadn't dealt with many foreigners, but there were a few that might be of some help if the money was sizable enough. There was a Rutger Bower in Germany. Victor had provided him with the documents when they denied him entry back into the country. Then there was Olaf Olofson, the Swedish swindler on the run, who took his clients for a billion dollars. He needed an alias passport in order to return home periodically to visit his family. And there was Heinrich Menschlouser. Mensch, he thought. Yes, he's the one who can do it. Mensch dealt in gunrunning and was always looking to make a dollar, honest or illegal–it didn't matter. If the price was right, he'd be interested.

"Yes, I think I can help you," Victor answered. "But I have to make a few phone calls first before I can say for sure. If it can be done, it will be expensive. Now, what kind?"

Charlie, not missing a beat, replied, "Two guns, forty or forty-five caliber, with silencers."

"Silencers? Now you're making a difficult situation even trickier."

"Vic, I have to have guns with silencers. Where these boys are going, they can't be makin' any noise. So what do you have to do to get 'em for me?"

"All right, got it. I'll get on it. How soon do you need them?"

"Well, my guys are a little tied up right now, but soon, soon, they'll be ready to head out." Charlie was careful with his words. He almost said, "Well, after they finish kicking some ass here, they'll be ready to head to another country and do the same thing!"

"Victor, a word of caution here," Charlie said in a serious tone–one not familiar to Victor. "For your own health," he continued, "don't let any of what I just told you leak out. My friends are dangerous, formidable men. They wouldn't hesitate to blow anyone apart, anyone who betrayed them."

Victor was normally a paid snitch. He wouldn't hesitate to sell information as important as this, but word on the street was that Kurt Morose had a contract on some old guy and a kid. Supposedly, Kurt's men missed their marks, and the marks had reversed the situation by killing eight of Kurt's men— mercenaries, it was said. Victor quickly put two and two together and couldn't help but wonder if these two friends of Charlie's were the same. After all, everyone knew that an old man lived in the back of the shop. Victor was a street guy. He'd been around the block and he was smart enough to play dumb and play it straight.

"Okay, Charlie," Victor said. "I'll get back to you as soon as I have something to tell you."

Chapter Twelve

Martha was beside herself with worry. She hadn't heard from Lom for some time now and she was sure that he had gotten himself into more trouble. Her imagination was running wild. There were people looking for him, and she feared the worst. For many years, Martha's sole concern was to support her children and be able to offer them an education that would give them a greater chance in life, to afford them opportunities that she had never had. There wasn't a single regret but, admittedly, there had been lonely times. The idea of male companionship was something that Martha had suppressed over the years. Fast forward to the present. Now, when she least expected it, she had met a man she really cared about. Never mind the nineteen-year age difference. That didn't matter, but what did matter was the fact that her love needed to get through this horrible nightmare ALIVE in order to realize her dream of the two of them together.

Martha couldn't stand it any longer. Right now, she would call Charlie. She needed to find out what was going on with Lom. Martha needed to know if he was safe. She needed to know now.

Martha called the pawnshop. Charlie picked up on the second ring. "Charlie's Pawnshop. How can I help you?"

"Charlie, it's Martha. I'm coming to the shop. It's about Lom. I have to know what's happening with him."

"Martha, it's not a good time. Just wait a while and I'll tell you everything," Charlie insisted.

"No," Martha argued. "Charlie, I'm coming to see you as soon as I finish my shift. If you're closed, open up when I knock. I'm having a hard time concentrating and need to have some answers."

Before Charlie could persist, Martha had hung up the phone. Charlie, staring at the phone, stood still for a minute, as if trying to decide what to do next. As he hung up the phone, he made a quick decision. He hung the "BE BACK IN 20 MINUTES" sign, locked his front door, and rushed up the snow-covered street to the diner to ward off Martha. Charlie walked up Second Avenue as fast as his skinny legs could take him. He was almost at the entrance of the Good Burger when the door opened and Martha walked out.

"Charlie, what are you doing here? I was just on my way to see you."

"Yeah, and that's exactly why I came here. You can't just be doing things on a whim, Martha. Everything Lom and me do, we plan before doing it. You might even say it's choreographed. We don't do nothing without thinking things out beforehand and by you walking in on us unannounced, it could just mess up the applecart. What's today? Tuesday? Wait 'til Friday, then come in pay me a visit. How's that sound?"

"Well, I don't know about that. What do you say we walk back into the restaurant and talk?"

"No good, Martha. I have to be getting back to my store. I'm expecting some people and that's why I didn't want you to be there. It could be dangerous for you and maybe me too if they tie you to Lom. Don't you see what I'm trying to tell ya?"

Martha hung her head in defeat. "I don't like it one bit, Charlie, but ... I don't want to do anything to get Lom hurt. Okay, I'll wait until Friday." She looked up at Charlie with tears in her eyes. "Charlie, I don't mean to be interfering with your plans, but I found out that I might love that old man and I want nothing to happen to him. You understand, don't you?"

She said it with such feeling that Charlie felt it too. "Now don't you go worrying, Martha. Lom knows what he's doing and I'll make sure and tell him you were asking about him 'cause you're worried that he might get himself hurt and all. Now you go home and don't worry about him. He'll be just fine and, when Friday comes around, then you just up and come see me. How's that sound?"

Charlie lifted Martha's chin. Tears were rolling down her face. He pulled her close to him. "Now, now, Martha. I told you Lom can take care of himself and he has Toby watching his back and he's got me to watch out for, because if he ever got hisself all shot up, I would stomp on his back like an elephant and he don't want any of that bad stuff to happen, so you know he's gonna take care of hisself."

Martha couldn't help laughing at the way Charlie was trying to make her feel better. She looked up at him and smiled. "Charlie, you have a way with words," she said. "An elephant stomping on his back." They both laughed at the ludicrousness of Charlie's words.

Still laughing, Charlie said to her, "Yeah, well, you get the meaning of what I'm trying to tell you."

"How can I not?" She laughed again. "Thank you, Charlie. That was sweet of you. The words, I mean. I won't bother you again until Friday."

"Go home now and I'll see you Friday morning."

Charlie and Martha turned and walked off in different directions–Martha to her house and Charlie to his store.

Talvania

Lars dialed a number on his cell phone. Becker picked up on the first ring. "Becker, could you please tell me what's going on in America? I need an update and, from now on, I want to be briefed on the status of my brother every morning. Do you understand? EVERY MORNING!"

Becker never liked to see Lars angry. There was no telling what he might do. He wished he had something positive to tell him. He thought about whether to tell him about the latest news he had received. Then he thought about the consequences he faced if the temporary King found out from another source, so he told Lars what he knew.

"Your Majesty, I heard from America just a little while ago." It wasn't exactly true. Becker had received a phone call at eight o'clock that morning. It was now ten twenty-five.

"The news is not good, Your Majesty. That old man killed four more men. The prey has become the hunter, Your Majesty. The old man is now stalking the leader of the ruffians we hired. If he is successful, that will clear the way for him and our target to come here and face you."

"That's insane," Lars snarled. "How could one young man and an old man possibly fight us to a successful conclusion? Tell me how, Becker! Please explain that to me so I can understand it. He's an old man, for God's sake. Well, so be it! If they have the nerve to come here to my palace, then they are obviously out of their minds. In fact, I hope they do come here. I'd like to face my brother right here in my castle, right where there's a place for those who don't understand conformity. He's my brother, so I'll be a little merciful, but I will pronounce a life sentence of hard labor right here in the dungeons. That should keep him quiet for a long time, don't you think, Becker?"

"Yes. Yes, Your Majesty. That certainly would keep him quiet. I would think forever," Becker replied.

The false King laughed. "I like that, Becker. That would give me great pleasure, knowing my brother is languishing in my dungeon while I am ruling his country, my country. It should have been my country all along. I'm the better leader.

Just imagine, Becker. All my life, I've taken a back seat, watching as he was being groomed for the throne and, all my life, I felt insignificant. Everything has always been Toby, Toby, Toby. All I wanted was just a little slice of the throne, just a little, but you know what? There is no such thing. It's all or nothing with the throne. All or nothing. Let the fool come. I'll be ready for him."

Becker felt much better, too. The queasiness in his stomach had gone and the false King was in a much better mood, much better than Becker expected.

Chapter Thirteen

"Toby, search all the men, living and dead, and take their weapons. Put them in the bag hanging in the corner," Lom instructed. The bag looked like a small flight bag with blue and red stripes on either side of it. Toby obediently collected the cell phones and the weapons, which included two ankle guns and a few knives. He gave all the wallets to Lom. Lom was struck by how much money these boys carried on them. He placed the cash on the table and divided it into the various denominations. Toby located some thick rubber bands and used those to bind and secure the bundles of cash. The two men placed the cash, together with the guns, into the flight bag. Lom kept the dead men's wallets, but returned the wallets to the guys he had shot in the knees.

"Help 'em up and over to a chair," Lom said to Toby, nodding toward the wounded, whining men. Toby shouldered one man, then the other, and guided them each to a seat.

Lom looked straight in the eyes of the larger of the two men and said, "I don't like hurting people like this. It doesn't make me feel good. But you fellas didn't leave me much of a choice now, did you?" The man opened his mouth to speak, but Lom quickly thrust out his hand, signaling him to be quiet. "I'm giving you back your wallet and credit cards, but I'm keeping the cash. I have a feeling I'm gonna be needing a lot of cash before we finish this little adventure of ours." Lom handed the man a cell phone. "Call your boss. Tell him I want to meet with him. Tell him I really don't relish the idea of killing him, but I will if I have to. I just want to end this animosity he has towards Toby, here and me. Now you dial him. Go ahead, dial him."

The man, grimacing in pain, looked at the phone and struggled to dial his boss. His voice trembling, he said, "Hello, Kurt. Larry. I have someone here who wants to speak with you." Lom grabbed the phone immediately.

"How are you?" Lom taunted sarcastically.

"Who's this?" the voice on the other end asked.

"This is the old man. I want to meet with you; have a little talk."

Ripples of fear shot down Kurt's spine. This wasn't something he normally experienced, especially given his work. Typically, Kurt was the one that everyone feared. He tried to gain his composure and asked in a somewhat calm voice, "How many of my men are dead this time?"

"Just two," Lom said nonchalantly. "The other two are fine—just a little shot up is all. They'll be okay in a month or two. Might not walk properly again, but they'll be okay. Now, do we meet, or do I just come over to your place and kill you? Which is it?"

"Christ, you sonofabitch. You killed fourteen of my men and you've seriously injured two others!"

Lom chimed in, "Well, that's not exactly accurate. I only killed thirteen. Somebody else killed the other one. Now, I think it would be better if we met because what you most likely don't know is that I've killed many more than this—not your men, but many, many others—so a few more notches on my gun won't affect my sleep one bit."

Kurt's mind raced with things he wanted to say, but didn't. This old man is brazen, he thought. His voice is as strong as steel. Who the hell does he think he is? Does he really think I'll cower?

"Well, that might be a good idea. You come to me." This was twisting into a poker game.

"Nah," Lom answered. "I don't think that's a good idea. The idea of committing suicide by foretold ambush doesn't really appeal to me. Hah, you must be kidding. How about this? We meet at the pawnshop–the place where you sent your guys to look for me in the beginning. It's neutral, and it's safe and it's a good place to settle our differences." Lom knew well that a man like Kurt would most likely not agree to such foolishness.

This was the old man's turf, the pawnshop, and Kurt would certainly much more prefer a place he could control. But that son of a bitch old man would not fall for such elementary tricks and Kurt knew it. Why, he wouldn't respect him if he did. If he wanted to end this bloodshed, he knew he'd have to agree to the old man's terms. He knew it and the words of Sun Tzu, in THE ART OF WAR, that he remembered when he was a young soldier, rang in his ears–"GENERALLY, HE WHO OCCUPIES THE FIELD OF BATTLE FIRST AND AWAITS THE ENEMY IS AT EASE; HE WHO COMES LATER TO THE SCENE AND RUSHES INTO THE FIGHT IS WEARY."

Chapter Fourteen

They set the meeting for Sunday morning at eleven a.m., but Kurt needed an edge. He sent two of his men to keep a lookout in the pawnshop area. He knew he had a clear advantage — they were coming to him. The hunt was over. The search would no longer require Kurt's men to feverishly hunting down Toby and Lom by combing the massive districts within New York City. It was a wait and see situation now. Kurt assigned his right-hand man, Chet, to supervise the operation. He was capable and professional. Kurt wanted no hiccups this time. If the old man showed up days early, they would just kill him and be done with it. If he showed up for the scheduled meeting, they'd kill him there. Either way, Kurt thought, this little saga was coming to a close.

Kurt's men waited impatiently all day Wednesday and Thursday. On Friday, early dawn, the girl from the restaurant showed up. Chet tried to figure out the significance of the woman being here. Why was she here? His mind raced. Did she have anything to hock, maybe a ring or a bracelet or some sort of jewelry in her bag? And if not, why would she be coming here this early in the morning? The more he thought about it, the more he became convinced that somehow, some way, this waitress was the key to finding the old man. Deep in thought, one of his men tried to get his attention. Chet raised his hand and said, "Quiet. I'm thinking." The men knew Chet and knew enough not to push it. They slouched back into their seats and resumed chit chat.

Okay, Chet reasoned as the damn thing kept nagging at him. The woman worked nights in the restaurant... the old man was a regular at the restaurant... the old man visited her on some nights.

"Aha," he said out loud. "That's it! Why didn't I think of that before?" he asked no one in particular.

His car companions looked up in bewilderment and dared to ask, "What? What is it? What?"

Could it be that simple, Chet thought? Chet was known for his hunches. It was those instincts that had brought many a man to his knees. Chet interrupted his men. "Look in the pawnshop and tell me what you see." They all stared that way.

"We're looking. What is it we're supposed to see?" the men answered.

"The woman in there. Do you see her?"

"Yeah. What about her?"

"I think she's connected to the old man somehow. I'm guessing she's his daughter or a niece or some other relative and, if I'm right, that gives us the edge we been looking for."

Martha barreled through the front door. Charlie, stunned, looked to see Martha standing there, all smiles. The color drained from his face.

"Hi, Charlie," she said. "Well..." she continued. Charlie hesitated a moment, not knowing exactly what to say without alarming her.

"Martha, I completely forgot about our appointment this morning. And I forgot to call you to tell you not to come. It's too dangerous right now, Martha, and right now, I'm afraid you need to just turn around and leave."

With her arms wrapped around her chest defiantly, she sternly replied, "I'm not going anywhere, Charlie, until you tell me what's going on."

"You know exactly what's going on, Martha. Men are trying to kill Lom and Toby and you being here doesn't help any. You best be going, you hear?"

"I'm not going anywh–" At that moment, the door flew open with a passion. Three men stormed in. As fast as a snake, one man picked up Martha as though she was a chair, lifted her high into the air, and headed for the door.

"Tell the old man we have his girl," the man smirked on his way out. "And if he wants her back, he's going to have to give us the kid. You tell him that. Understand?"

"Put me down," Martha said as she kicked and screamed. "Charlie, Charlie! Help! Let go of me!" she squealed until the man holding her placed a firm hand over her mouth, silencing her.

The door was still half ajar when Charlie picked up the radio and clicked it twice. "Lom here."

"Lom, they came in here and got Martha."

"Martha! What in the hell was she doing there?" Lom yelled.

"She wanted to come in earlier in the week, but I put her off 'til today, thinking we would have the problem all worked out, but I forgot to call her and cancel our appointment for this morning. She came in and wanted to know what was happening. Now they have her. They came in and took her just like that. Picked her up like she was a feather. Told me to tell you that if you want her back, give up Toby."

"They said that, did they?" Lom answered in the meanest voice Charlie had ever heard out of Lom. "Well, that just settles it. I'm just gonna have to get her, even if it means killing some more of them. These fellas just don't seem to get it, do they? Well, I better sign off for now. I have a lot of thinking to do. But you can bet on one thing, Charlie. Before this night is over, I'll either have Martha or I'll be dead." The two-way radio got quiet and Charlie just stared at its silence for a few moments, turned it off, and in slow motion, slowly and gently laid it on his desk.

Toby had been listening to both ends of the conversation.

"Toby, you heard what I said?"

"Yes, I heard everything," Toby answered.

"Well," Lom said. "I'm going to get her back. You feel like tagging along for another ride?"

Toby smiled and said, "I wouldn't have it any other way. I haven't had this much excitement in my entire life. And you know, Lom, when I was being hunted, I never thought I would live through the night, and now we're the ones doing the hunting–aiming for the guys who are trying to kill me. Of course, I'll come. You need some manpower."

Lom smiled that lopsided smile of his. He had become fond of this boy. He had grit, and he was dependable. Lom had thought of him as a son. He felt a kinship to him and he didn't want this boy harmed. Once this was over, and he was sure it would be soon, then they would make plans to go back to his country and take back the throne from his brother Lars. Yes siree. That's what they'd do.

Lom sat at the table and thought for a moment, then he looked at Toby and said, "Toby, would you bring me the wallets we took off of those fellas yesterday? I took their money and credit cards out, but I didn't check to see if there were any addresses listed anywhere. Something might give us a clue where they took Martha. It wasn't important yesterday, but could be now."

Toby walked toward the table, picked up the wallets, and handed them to Lom. Lom examined them carefully. He pulled out every loose piece of paper, every business card, every dollar bill, every receipt, and placed them into one small heap on the table.

"A full wallet is like a lady's handbag," Lom stated without looking up. "It accumulates things and, before you know it, the wallet becomes as fat as a blowfish." Lom pushed the empty wallets to the side and began sifting through the small accumulation. He separated them into three piles.

He picked up the receipts first and checked dates, items, times, and places. He found nothing, not a hint. Next, he lifted the slips of paper and read the scribble. Nothing. He went back over the slips a second time, hoping he had missed something, carefully rotating each paper. He held them to the light, searching for anything, anything at all. Still nothing.

Next were the business cards. Lom separated the cards that he deemed "might have some potential." The worthless ones he threw into the garbage can, along with the other papers and receipts. There was one remaining stack. Lom combed through it, letter by letter, looking for clues or codes, something. Aggravated, he threw half of those away as well. There were only six cards left. He narrowed those down to two, discarding another two. He studied both cards quietly, intently. One card was from a parking garage in midtown Manhattan. Lom wondered why someone would keep a card from a parking garage. That question warranted that card a "keeper." The second card had a business name, address, and phone number on the front with a handwritten phone number on the back.

"Camfield Waste Management," Lom said aloud. "There's an address in Brooklyn," he said as he handed the card to Toby. "Stay here a moment while I get to a pay phone."

Lom set off down the promenade of the abandoned station and made his way to the Forty-Second Street Station. Careful not to be noticed, he stepped onto the platform and melded into the crowd. In the distance, he spotted a pay phone. He took his place behind the caller, but the caller was taking his time. Lom shuffled his feet, coughed, and paced a little in order to make the caller uncomfortable. The caller finally got the hint and ended his conversation. Lom dialed the number on the front of the card. "Camfield Waste Management," a woman's voice answered. "How may I direct your call?"

"I'm sorry," Lom said. "I must have dialed a wrong number." The card was legitimate, it seemed.

As he was about to walk away, Lom remembered the handwritten phone number on the back. He dialed it and a man answered on the first ring. "Kurt here." Bingo! Lom smiled.

"Kurt," Lom said. "This is the old man. How nice it is to hear your voice this fine morning." Kurt stared at the phone and fell silent. How the hell did this happen?

Chapter Fifteen

"Kurt, are you still on the phone?" Lom asked.

Kurt, still a bit dumbfounded, replied, "Yes, I'm here."

"Good, Mr. Kurt, because I want to add a little something to our deal that we have happening on Sunday."

"What little thing are you talking about?"

"That woman you took from Charlie's pawnshop. I want you to let her go. I don't particularly like getting innocent people involved in my business. She's just a waitress who works hard, and she doesn't know a thing about any of this."

"Well, old man," Kurt said condescendingly. "Chet thinks maybe you might know each other, and if that's the case speaking of pawnshops, she just may be my pawn." He laughed, proud of his little joke. "What do you think that pawn guy would give me for her? Get it? You have the King, I have the pawn, and I'm about to check your King with my pawn." Kurt laughed again. He was on a roll.

Lom wasn't laughing. "I want you to let her go."

"I will not do that, Mr. Old Man. The lady stays. Now, I want the King. When I get HIM, you get HER. Understand?"

"Well," Lom said. "I guess I do. Well, now, I believe maybe we will not be meeting on Sunday. Am I correct in thinking that, Kurt?"

Kurt thought for a moment. Maybe the meeting should take place now that he was in a position of power. He had the woman, a woman that the old man seemed soft on and Kurt still didn't have the King. "No sense canceling the meeting after all the trouble we had in setting it up. So why not have it?"

"Tell you what, Kurt," Lom said sternly. "I'm not gonna kill you today, but understand something–no one hurts one of my friends without dying afterwards. You're a dead man, Kurt. And you're the only one who doesn't seem to know it. I'll see you on Sunday if you're still alive then." Lom hung up the phone. Until now, he hadn't shown his vulnerable side, but Kurt had clearly hit him where it hurt. It was hard to smile. Lom was concerned.

Kurt's hand was shaking as he hung up his phone. It finally set in. As much as he didn't want to believe it, he was no longer in control. For the first time, the tables had clearly turned. This old man was a cocky son of a bitch. Could the guy actually get to him? He had somehow peeled off several of Kurt's finest. Kurt's face flushed as he thought of this little old man penetrating Kurt's insulators. He was a bit disarmed by all of it. A chill marched down his spine–one just like the ones he had felt before.

"Chet," Kurt called. Chet entered Kurt's makeshift office and took a seat on the other side of the desk, facing his boss. "How many men do we still have?" Kurt asked.

"Well," Chet paused. "The old man has killed fourteen of our boys."

Kurt jumped out of his comfortable leather chair. "Goddamnit, Chet. I didn't ask you how many men he's killed. I asked you how many men we still have!"

Chet thought for a moment. "We have six men out in the warehouse and another six men still looking for them. That gives us twelve men, not counting us."

"What about the Russians?" Kurt asked.

"They're gone. There's nothing in it for them and no motivation to stay. They know that fourteen men got killed by this guy and when we did nothing about it, they didn't see an upside–no reason to stay. They left."

"So, didn't you offer them enough money? It's all about the payoff, Chet! Everything, everything's about the money! What don't you get, you dumb shit?"

Chet didn't take kindly to being insulted and, raising his voice, yelled back, "How much is enough, Kurt? Huh? How much? There were ten Russians! If we paid them each twenty-five grand, that'd be a quarter of a million dollars... just to hunt down one old man and a kid. If we can't do it ourselves, what makes you think a bunch of Russians can? And if that old man kills them, we'll have the rest of the Russians all over our asses! I DIDN'T and DON'T think the risk is worth the reward."

Chet's words resonated. It made sense. "Okay, okay. I get it! Maybe you made the right decision," Kurt said. "If we can't do it on our own, we appear weak to the Russians, and before you know it, they could get ideas and move in on us. Okay. Call all our boys in. Get them back here. Who knows what this crazy old bastard will do next? He just might be nuts enough to get me here. The old man said he was going to kill me. He said I was a dead man, that I didn't know it yet. This guy actually sounds like he can do it. Well, hell, he's proven some things already. I just don't get it. How the hell can a little old man wreak such havoc on trained mercenaries and smile while he's doing it? I think he's a damn psycho and those are the ones you have to look out for."

Lom and Toby walked through the subway and straight to the ladder that would lead them to the hidden floor entrance in Charlie's pawnshop. When they reached the top of the ladder, the metal trapdoor wouldn't budge. They banged their knuckles until they were bruised and knocked loudly. It still wouldn't open. Lom took his knife out and banged with the handle. After a few unsuccessful attempts and many minutes later, the cover lifted and there stood Charlie.

"Sorry about the delay, fellas," Charlie said. "I put a bolt through the cover so I wouldn't get any unexpected visitors. I didn't expect to see you tonight. Why didn't you use the radio I gave you?"

"Because I just plum forgot about the stupid thing. I forgot– that's why I didn't call you. Is that excuse enough for you?" Lom snapped. Lom's mind was fixated on Martha and, at the moment, was one story short on the elevator.

"Now don't you go get your dander up with me," Charlie answered. "I ain't gonna take it from a no-account, ole fart like you." Charlie looked at Lom. "Well, what is it you want from me now, Lom?"

"Now that you brought it up," Lom replied. "I could use a favor. We need to get in touch with that handy contact of yours at the telephone company. Can you call him again and get an address from this phone number?" He handed him the card with the written phone number on it.

"I sure can," Charlie answered. "I'll call him right now while you're waiting."

In a matter of minutes, Charlie had an address he had scribbled on the back of a pawn receipt. "Here ya go." Lom studied it for a moment. The address was in Queens.

"Thanks a bunch, Charlie. With a little luck, we might end this tonight. I just don't see this going on beyond Sunday, but you never know."

Lom and Toby wasted no time. Martha was in danger. They scampered like little rats back down the ladder, disappearing so fast, it made Charlie dizzy. Charlie waited for a moment, bolted the door again, and pulled the rug back over the secret entrance. He unlocked the front door just as a customer was entering with a handful of jewelry.

Back at the hideout, Lom sat at the table, contemplating the two addresses. It was a fifty-fifty shot. He could go back to the warehouse in Brooklyn or he could check out this new address in Queens. New fallen snow had become a problem. Taking a car was out of the question. Luckily, the trains were running on a steady schedule, so once again, they opted for the subway. Toby and Lom took the IRT Flushing Line. It was originally called the Woodside and Corona Line at the Forty-Second Street Station. It was one of two lines of the New York City subway system to have been operated by two distinct divisions: the IRT and BMT. The two men took the Seven train to Willets Point Station, the place originally built for the nineteen thirty-nine World's Fair and used again for the nineteen sixty-four World's Fair. Today, they mostly used it for events at the U.S. Tennis Center on the south side of the tracks and for baseball games at the new Mets City Stadium on the north side.

The men got off at Willets Point and walked toward Flushing. What should have been a short walk took much longer because of the heavy snow. They eventually came to a series of junkyards that stood on both sides of Roosevelt Avenue under the El. Judging by the number, the address they were looking for should be on the right side of the street. The two men walked slowly, trying not to look suspicious. They were the only bodies lurking in this desolate part of the avenue, traipsing through the heavy snow. A few cars, braving the weather, passed, but there were no other pedestrians–just Lom and Toby. Each man took turns checking behind them, their vision limited by the heavy falling powder. There was some comfort knowing they were the only persons walking in this snowstorm in either direction. They were the only two souls crazy enough to be out in this weather, and surely they had to stand out should someone be watching them. Lom pulled his silenced PPKS from his pocket and held it close to his leg. He wanted to feel its security, even though his fingers were freezing. The weather was becoming their ally because it hid them from anyone who dared to venture out on this horrible, snowy night. While it wasn't snowing as hard as it was the night Toby escaped from Kurt's killers, it was still snowing hard enough to prevent seeing twenty feet ahead. Lom liked it. It reminded him of his time in Korea. Toby liked it because it reminded him of Talvania. And they both liked it because of the cover it afforded them. There was a downside, however. Trying to make out addresses was tough. The accumulation of snow had coated some numbers and without walking up to each one individually, it was tricky. They developed a system–spotting one address. They began counting off the other front yards until they felt they were in the vicinity. The cold made the walk seem eternal. Minutes passed until they came to the entrance of a junkyard. The address dangling from the chain-link gate guarding it matched the one Charlie had given them. The men almost missed it. A jeep, parked close by, was partially blocking the numbers and the gate.

Lom was eager to get inside the building. Number one, he was freezing and, number two, he had business to finish. The men slipped past the jeep. They looked in amazement at the gate, ajar, with the lock unsecured. It was as if the gate was welded into the position by the snow mounds on each side.

Spotting the address yet again on the building, Lom said, "Yep, this is the place." Old cars and junk parts filled each space–cars and vehicles that were once new had come here to die, or to be refurbished, over time, into perhaps something once again valuable. Ducking along the way, Toby and Lom made their way to the right side of the building–the area least cluttered. They crept slowly, lightly placing each foot into the virgin snow, careful not to step too quickly for fear of the sound of crunching snow giving away their presence. Suddenly, the front door opened, and a man exited onto a snowy path, then through the gate. He jumped into the four-wheel-drive jeep and slowly drove away.

Lom and Toby made their way along the wall to the rear of the building. Maybe they'd be as lucky as they were the other night and gain entrance through the back door, Lom thought.

That idea was thwarted. The back door was solid steel, and it appeared to be shiny and brand new. Lom guessed that they have installed this door within the last few days. Further down on the other side of the building there was a Bilco door leading to the basement, which was unlocked, and they could access the building.

A stairway stood diagonally opposite them and they made their way toward it. As they passed through the middle of the room, a tarp nesting in the center moved. Lom reached for his gun and took aim. The tarp moved again. Lom motioned to Toby to cover him and, in one swift motion, he pulled off the tarp. To their amazement, there was Martha, staring up at them, all bound up and looking like the Tinman, smothered in gray from head to toe. The men worked quickly to remove the duct tape. Just as they removed the last piece, the cellar door opened. There was no time for all three to make it to the boiler near the window. Grasping the duct tape, Lom motioned for Toby to take the tarp and place it over himself. Lom grabbed Martha's hand and guided her to the boiler. They crouched behind it, sucking in their breath so as not to make a sound.

The stranger hesitated on the top step for a moment, turned, and yelled to his buddies. "How many beers do you want?"

A voice yelled back. "Bring up a six-pack."

"Okay," the man answered back.

"Oh, and check on the princess while you're down there," a voiced yelled from upstairs.

Lom trained his gun on the canvas.

From the stairs, the man eyed Martha's tarp in the middle of the room. Satisfied that she was still secured, he went to the refrigerator and pulled out six cans of beer. As he was making his way back to the stairs, he tapped the tarp with his feet in order to taunt her. The tarp shook in protest. The man smiled and yelled up to his buddies, "I checked on her. She's alive and kicking."

Martha and Lom watched the man ascend the stairs. When the door closed behind him, Lom rushed over and pulled the tarp off of Toby. "Come on; let's get out of here," Lom said. "Sorry to have you do that, Toby, but I was ready for him."

Toby was halfway to the door when Martha, who was following him, remembered she hadn't taken her bag with her and she went back for it. With her bag securely on her shoulder, Lom took her arm and together they navigated through the dark, crowded cellar and up the stairs toward the door. When Martha and Lom were safely outside, Lom closed the Bilco door quietly behind him and the three of them walked to the gate. Lom walked backwards, still in motion while watching the front door, with his gun pointed as steady as could be, making sure there were no surprise visitors following. They squeezed past the open gate and sped up their pace as best they could, given the weather, trotting all the way to the Willets Point train station. It was desolate, making it easier for Lom to keep his hands on his gun. He watched one side of the station while Toby covered the other. The Flushing train slid into the station and screeched to a halt — safety and warmth at last.

Chapter Sixteen

Lom trailed behind Martha and Toby throughout the long walk to the little known entrance leading to the underground hideaway. They walked along the side of the tunnel, staying close to the wall. Lom kept reminding them of that dreaded third rail, warning them that no matter what happened, never to jump onto the tracks, even if they were vacant. Each time they heard the rails clack, it was a signal that a train was coming, and each time, Lom yanked on both Toby and Martha, backing them into another worker's alcove. The tunnel was dark, and Martha quickly vocalized her fear of the dark and her fear of rats. She envisioned Norwegian sewer rats running up her legs. She cringed at each little sound. Lom, unbeknownst to her, smiled each time. He liked it. He was her protector. Lom wanted to be her protector.

It was twenty-five minutes later when they reached the steps, hidden by darkness. Lom shined his penlight and guided Martha up the stairs. What she saw underneath the Manhattan streets amazed her.

"What is this place, Lom? It's beautiful, but it's scary. Look at the posters. My God, they date back to the second World War."

"Come on, Martha. We have to get to safety. Right now, we're wide open and we're sitting ducks," Lom cautioned.

They walked along the side of the wide promenade, past stores that hadn't been used in over sixty years. It was eerie, Martha thought, this graveyard of abandoned stores. As they approached their destination, Lom stopped, reached into his pocket, and pulled out a set of keys. He searched for the right one, found it, and inserted it into the lock.

"Madame," Lom said. "Welcome to Lom's hideout."

They walked through the empty store and stepped into the back room. Lom hit a switch and light filled the room. It pleasantly surprised Martha to see modern conveniences. Lom showed her where the coffee was, pointed out the hot and cold water, and the bathroom. Lom put on a pot of coffee and waited for it to percolate. He placed three cups on the table. Toby set cream and sugar alongside a plate of doughnuts.

Lom grinned and said, "It's not dinner, but it tastes good and, in a pinch, it'll do."

Martha smiled back. She felt safe. "Lom, Toby, I didn't have time to thank you. How on earth did you know where to find me when I didn't even know where I was? "

"Truth is, we got lucky, Martha," Lom answered. He took this opportunity to tell her how they could find her and about the men they had killed and wounded. "We found a card in a wallet from one of the dead men that had a penciled number written on it. It was easy–almost too easy. We called the numbers on the front of the card first to find out they were legitimate. Then we called the number on the back of the card and we hit the jackpot. I called the number and Kurt picked up."

"Excuse me. Who's Kurt?"

"He's the boss man of this bunch of misfits. On a hunch, I had Charlie have his nephew check out the address that belongs to the phone number and it came back with the address where we found you. We did not know we would find you in that place. I figured on us going upstairs and killing a few of those boys–thought that the ones left would give us some information where you were being held. But since we found you, those boys will live another day now. Now, if you'll excuse me, I have to make an important phone call."

Martha looked quizzically at Lom. "Who are you going to call at this time of the night?"

Lom charmed Martha with that half-cocked smile of his. "Why, I'm gonna call Kurt. I don't think he knows he doesn't own you any longer. I don't think the boys at the junkyard know it, either." Lom looked sheepishly at Martha. "Martha, honey, you wouldn't have a cell phone on you, would you?"

"It's a good thing I remembered to take my bag with me," she said. "Here, call that Kurt fellow." It thrilled Lom to see that deep down in this dungeon environment, he had a cell signal. He was grateful not to have to walk along the tracks to get to the Forty-Second Street Station pay phone. For the second time that day, he dialed Kurt's number. He winked at Martha and said, "Kurt's gonna think I'm a wizard finding you. One minute the guy checks on you and you're there, and the next minute you're gone. Yep, he's gonna go crazy wondering how."

Kurt picked up on the second ring. "Who the hell is calling me at this time of the night?"

"Calm down, Mr. Kurt, it's only me, your friendly little old man, calling."

"You again. What do you want now? Your girlfriend? Ha! Well, you can't have her. What do ya think of that?"

"Well, why in God's name would I want her when I already have her?"

"Ha ha, yeah, sure. Okay, you have her. Tell me another story. You are crazy."

"Well, you just might want to call your friends at that old junkyard. You might do them a favor because I don't think they know she's gone yet either. Go ahead. I'll be glad to hold while you make that call."

Lom heard the phone click as Kurt placed him on hold or hit the mute button. He couldn't tell which. Cautiously checking his battery, Lom waited patiently. A few minutes later, Kurt returned to the phone.

"Who the hell are you, old man? Who are you really? No one pulls this stuff on me and gets away with it! No one! So tell me who I'm dealing with? Are you with the government?"

"Nope," Lom answered. "But I will tell you I'm your worst nightmare, although you already know that, don't you? Well, don't worry about that 'cause you're gonna be a dead man soon."

"What do you want?" Kurt barked.

"What do I want? Well, let's start with this. If you want to live, just pay attention. It's really simple. You do as I say, and I'll forgive you for trying to kill me. But if you're lying to me, I'll sneak right up on you in the middle of the night and I'll make sure that you see my face. I'll talk to you a bit and then I'll shoot you right between the eyes. I want it all to stop. Call off your minions. Leave us all alone. I've got my sights on that Chet fella and the rest of your men, and that's a promise. Now what's it to be? Do we have a deal?"

"Old man, I would love to end this nightmare, but they paid me good money to kill that kid and I can't give the money back, so that puts us back to square one."

"Now hold on one minute, Kurt. Let me understand this. You can't stop pursuing us because they paid you a lot of money to kill Toby here? And I got in the way, so you have to kill me too. Am I right so far?"

"Right... so far."

"Okay then. I have an answer to your problem. If they've paid you and you having to give it back is the problem, what if you don't have to repay that money? Would you leave us alone then? Would that work for you?" Lom reasoned.

"Well, yeah. Well, no, because I still have a reputation to uphold, but that would definitely take the pressure off of me."

"Kurt, you don't scare me, but I'm looking for a reason not to have to kill you because it's just aggravating and I am really getting a little too old to be aggravated. So in order to avoid these unpleasantries, how's this? I take Toby back to his country and make sure he's recognized as the King."

"Yeah, and how do you plan on doing that?" Kurt asked sarcastically.

"I'm gonna go there and do what I have to do. I can do it. Do you agree? Do you agree I can do that? Help me out. I kinda lost count here. How many men went down on your end over this nonsense?" he asked.

"Sixteen," Kurt responded. "But who's counting?"

"Well, whatever. Now if I go over there and take care of some things, then there will be nobody left for you to pay money to–no debtors means no debt, right? Wouldn't that end your little contract?"

"Well yeah. If there's no one to answer to and no one to give money back to, then yes, the contract would be over."

"Then why don't we do this? Give me some time to get to Toby's country and straighten out a few things and, if I fail, which I hardly ever do, well, I guess we'll have to resume our little feud and I'll just have to come back here and kill you and the rest of your men. Does that sound like a fair deal to you?"

"Let me get this straight. You want me to back off and let you take Toby back to his country, where you can kill everyone who is against the real king, including the person who hired me?"

"Yep. That's pretty much it. Oh, and one more thing. I want nothing to happen to Martha while I'm away. I would be furious if I returned to find her hurt, or missing, or harmed in any way–any of those nasty happenings. Now I need your word on that."

"Nothing will happen to her, old man. There is nothing to gain by hurting her and everything to lose. It's a bad business move to hurt her, so don't worry about it. Just do what you say and we'll call it even. Although, when this is all over, I would like to meet you. I'll be honest with you. I kinda admire you. You almost put me out of business. But that's just business and

I don't hold it against you. Meet me anywhere you say. Pick a place where you know you'll be safe. I'd really like to meet you, see your face, shake your hand, and that's the truth. I've never come across anyone who could put fear into me like you did–just for a moment, mind you, but you did it. Would you do that?"

"Well, I don't see why not. We both have nothing to gain by killing anymore and who knows, maybe we might get to like one another, maybe be kinda friends and when I make friends, I make 'em for life. Yeah, I'll do that just as soon as I kill a bunch of those people who are looking to hurt Toby. We'll have that little get together so I can give you the news that you don't owe anyone anything. How's that sound?"

Kurt relaxed a bit. He really wanted this chapter to end, and the old man seemed to have a perfect solution. If he successfully accomplished what he said, then all of Kurt's problems would be over. He wouldn't have to return any of the money and he would keep what was left of the two million dollars... IF the old man could pull it off. He really didn't want this old man hunting him. For a few moments, Kurt felt the pressure leave his body. The thought of walking away alive, with a lot of money, as unrealistic as it might seem, was thrilling.

Kurt picked up the phone and called his men, one by one, ordering them to stand down. The story was the same–the old man, and the kid were not their problems any longer, at least for now. The contract was off. They cancelled the hit on the kid and it was back to business as usual.

Kurt was too wired to return to bed. Instead, he ambled over to his home bar, poured himself a scotch and water, and relaxed into his recliner. He smiled as his head swirled with thoughts of this old guy–so smart, so ballsy. He had to admit that he liked the guy. Never in his life had he met anyone like him. The man just didn't rattle. He was so sure of himself and his ability. This old man had discovered all of Kurt's hideouts and had even stolen back the girl with no one knowing it. Could he do it? Could the old man travel to a foreign country, a place like Talvania, and kill everyone who wanted to hurt the kid? Kurt laughed as he took another sip of his drink. "I'll bet that old son of a bitch pulls this off." He raised his glass and said, "Here's to you, old man. Here's to your success." He lifted his glass to his lips, drained it, and slowly drifted off to sleep.

Chapter Seventeen

The gang, including Martha, congregated in Charlie's pawnshop. There was a crazy celebratory mood. Beer was flowing. The group eagerly awaited Victor's arrival. Shortly after nine in the evening, Victor walked in, two of his men following close behind him. Victor was an intimidating presence. He was tall. He hid his girth under an expensively tailored suit. Victor was light on his feet for a big man and if you pulled him away from business talk, he was actually pleasant company. The problem was he was always talking, always looking for a business deal, and today was no different. He looked at the old man and the kid and then at Martha, and he nodded his approval.

"Charlie, I have those items you asked me to get for you," Victor announced. "Can we discuss this in your office?"

"Well, hell, Victor, you saw the pictures of my friends you made those things for, so why be bashful around them?" Victor was a little surprised. He didn't like witnesses in the middle of a business deal. Charlie sensed his hesitation.

"Okay, Victor. Let's go into my office for a few moments and conduct a little business," Charlie added. With the door firmly closed, Victor reached into his coat pocket, pulled out an envelope, and handed it to Charlie. Charlie pulled out the passports and placed the on his desk. The workmanship impressed him.

"Victor," Charlie said. "I've seen phony passports before, but these are works of art." Victor smiled at the compliment.

"Yes, they came out rather nice, didn't they?" Victor then reached into his other jacket pocket and pulled out another envelope. "This will take care of the guns you wanted. A man will meet you at the airport. His name is Heinrich Menschlouser, but he prefers to be called Mensch. I did some business with Mensch in the past and he's agreed to help you, for a fee, of course – a very large fee."

"Who do I pay? You or Mensch?"

"You owe me ten thousand for the passports and ten thousand for getting you the guns. You'll pay me my fee of twenty thousand dollars now, of course," Victor stated firmly.

"Aren't you forgetting about the credit cards I gave you?" Charlie reminded him.

"Of course not. They're included in the deal."

Charlie chuckled and said, "But of course."

Charlie walked to his safe and removed a stuffed envelope. Before handing it to Victor, he asked, "Did you get the silencers?"

"Yes, but that's another ten grand. Silencers are scarce."

"So, how much do I owe him?"

"He says twenty thousand–ten for the guns and ten for the silencers."

"How about ammunition?"

"I spoke to him about it. He'll give you ammo at no charge when he gives you the guns."

Charlie, appearing a little emotional, tugged on Victor's arm and said, "Victor, I really appreciate you doing this for us. I won't forget it and neither will my friends. That young fella out there is the true King of Talvania and before we leave that place, me and Lom will see him sitting on that throne. Come on; I want to introduce you to him. Maybe someday you and him could do a little legitimate business. You'll notice I emphasized the word 'legitimate.'"

Victors eyes lit up. He really hadn't thought of it that way. He knew an opportunity when he heard it. Victor knew about the dead men. A man like Victor had people on the streets, contacts everywhere. Not much escaped him. It was all out in the open now and he knew the King would be grateful to anyone who had helped him survive his ordeal. This one shady deal might lead to the business deal of all deals.

"Did you hear what I just said, Victor?" Charlie asked, jolting Victor back from his daydreams.

"Yeah, sorry. My mind went elsewhere for a while, took a brief vacation to Talvania." He chuckled. "But I heard what you said, Charlie. I'm looking forward to meeting the King."

Toby watched as the two men approached him. "Victor, I want to introduce you to the King of Talvania, Torbjorn Vorland."

Toby knew that when Charlie used his formal name, he should act the part.

"Your Highness," Charlie said. "Let me introduce you to a friend of mine, the one who worked a minor miracle securing these passports." Charlie reached into his pocket and handed a passport to the King. "This is yours, Your Majesty."

Toby opened the passport, and the quality of the work amazed him. The picture and the passport looked as if they issued them that way.

"I'm in your debt, Victor. When I regain the throne, you might visit our country. There may be some business opportunities for you there. Besides, I'm sure you will like Talvania. The climate is wonderful." It thrilled Victor with the invitation, and he was sure he had heard a hint of a business proposition. Toby nodded his head at Victor and gave him a slight bow as a sign of respect. He smiled, turned, and walked away to rejoin Lom.

Victor took Charlie's hand, shook it vigorously, and thanked him. "I owe you big time for this one, Charlie. I think me and the King will do business soon, thanks to you." Victor drifted over to the table where drinks were waiting and poured himself a short vodka tonic and raised his glass to the King. He placed the empty glass on the table and put on his heavy winter coat. He knew this wasn't his party, so he said his goodbyes. Victor settled into the back seat of his Lincoln town car and tried to get his head around who he had just met. He had just met a king–the King of Talvania.

Chapter Eighteen

The Three Musketeers–Charlie, Toby, and Lom –sat at the table lined with liquor. Lom spoke up and said simply, "It's time." The other two men nodded in agreement. "Are you ready to take back your throne, Toby?" Lom asked.

"I've never been more ready. Let's do it or die trying," Toby responded with a look of determination that brought a smile to the old man's wrinkled face.

"Well said, lad. Then let's get to finalizing our plan."

Charlie interrupted. "If'n you two amateurs think you're gonna go to Talvania without me, think again. Understand?"

Lom chimed in, "Now, wherever did you get the idea that you weren't part of my plan? In fact, you're a very important part of this plan, so no need for any unnecessary lip."

Charlie sank back in his seat, nodding in approval. He looked over at Lom. "Okay, so what exactly is the plan, YOUR PLAN… or do you even have one?"

"I have one, all right. My plan is this. We have our phony passports and—"

Charlie interrupted, "But why did you need phony passports? Why not use your regular passport? I know that you have one, so why not use that one?"

"Simple, Charlie. I plan on killing some people over in Talvania, and I can't use my regular passport in case I'm caught. Toby here has to use the phony one to get himself into his country, with no one recognizing him. I know for a fact that these people will wait for some kind of move from Toby here. They just don't know what it will be and that will work to our advantage. Lars will no doubt have men waiting at the airport. Now here's what we're gonna do. We're gonna fly into Talvania as a bunch of old tourists looking to have a good time just sight-seeing. Who's gonna think twice about two old men taking their grandson or nephew or whatever on a vacation? We're gonna walk in there and take back Toby's throne for him. In order to do that, we're gonna have to disguise Toby a bit, maybe get him a Yankee ball cap. Toby, stop shaving. You need to get some fuzz on your face, and if it isn't enough, we'll back it up by getting a mustache and a beard from one of those costume shops around here. We'll find you some touristy looking clothes. That should do the trick, but we don't want you looking raggedy or seedy. What we want is for you to look like an American tourist and, above all, you must look like this passport photo. We have a pile of dough from the guys we killed, so we might as well put it to good use and buy the things we need."

The three men talked well into the night. They discussed various scenarios on how to get into the castle, who would stand where, the signals they'd use, and what each meant. Toby gave them every detail of the building, the names of each guard, each staff worker. They quizzed each other, ensuring each person agreed. In the wee hours of the morning, Lom seemed satisfied with the final plan. The three men, not trusting Kurt's word and fearing that he might renege on their agreement, returned to their hideout in the abandoned train station. They slept soundly for the first time in weeks.

The fragrant aroma of Lom's fresh coffee woke Charlie and Toby. The men scarfed down the leftover donuts and bagels from the night before. Lom took out the passports and studied them carefully. He couldn't risk a snafu at customs.

"Whatcha' looking at, Lom?" Charlie asked.

"Just checking the pictures and the names we'll be using. Toby's name on his passport here is James Reagan. It's a pretty good fit. This name is suitable for his light hair and fair features. My name is Thomas Dorchester. That name will do me just fine." Lom looked at Charlie and asked, "You got the plane tickets like I told you... right?"

Charlie smiled. "Yep. Got three first-class, round-trip tickets. Never know. We might have to bring Toby back with us."

"You ornery old coot–you got three tickets figuring you were coming all along. You had it all planned." Lom turned to Toby. "You see, Toby, you can't trust anybody, especially an old codger who goes by the name of Charlie. I don't know what I'm gonna do with him when we get back. Looks like I can't even trust my best friend."

Toby loved the interaction between these two old men. It was amusing. These two old friends were entertaining–just like the old court jesters, Toby thought.

In New York City, the world is your oyster. One didn't have to walk very far to find whatever was needed. The men bought dress slacks, dress shirts, and sports jackets. Charlie supplied them with military gear–boots, camo shirts, and pants. They checked their lists, rechecked their belongings, and decided they were ready.

Once in the air, the three men got some well-deserved sleep. A pretty Talvania Airlines flight attendant wheeled by her cart and offered beverages. It was six in the morning and breakfast was being served. They had been flying for eight hours with another two to go.

A few minutes past eight a.m., the plane landed smoothly and taxied to its designated gate. Lom, Toby, and Charlie followed the signs leading to customs and endured the normal customs questions–business or pleasure, how long are you staying, etc. Everything went well, almost too easy. Done–the stamp of Talvania hammered down on each passport and the men proceeded toward baggage claim. If the false King had men watching the terminal, they would see two old men and a typical American youth wearing his Yankee baseball cap backwards. Nothing suspicious. While waiting at the luggage carousel, Lom noticed a man holding a sign with the name Dorchester on it. He told the boys to monitor the carousel while he stepped away for a moment.

The chauffeur smiled as Lom approached him. "Mr. Dorchester?" he asked.

"Yes, I'm Mr. Dorchester."

"I'm pleased to meet you, Mr. Dorchester," the man standing next to him said. "I'm Heinrich Menschlouser, but everyone knows me as Mensch."

"Well, I'm very pleased to meet you, Mr. Mensch."

"Just plain Mensch will do. When you get your luggage, my car is right outside. It's the American car, the black Lincoln."

The baggage area was quite efficient and didn't take long. Toby whispered that this was something he had worked on as King in order to promote tourism in his country. The airport and its fluidity were the first point of contact for most visitors and he wanted the first impression to be a good one.

The three men climbed into the back of the Lincoln. Mensch sat in the passenger's seat while his chauffeur drove. "I've taken the liberty to book you into one of the finest hotels in Talvania, the Trump Talvania. Just enjoy the scenery for now. We will talk business when we're in your hotel room, if that meets with your approval."

Charlie and Lom took in the sights and the beauty of the country as the luxurious Lincoln glided on a road leading to the castle. It was as Toby had described it—beautiful white buildings overlooking a cobalt blue sea. Everything seemed so peaceful. Once in a while, Toby would point out a special landmark or historic site. When they entered the city limits, the men were awed by the architectural beauty of the Talvanian whitewashed buildings that encompassed the city.

Toby tugged at Lom's shoulder and directed his attention to a large, magnificent structure in the distance. "That is my castle," Toby whispered to him.

The car neared a hotel built on a cliff overlooking the sea that was relatively close to the castle. Lom and Charlie were busy eyeing distances, openings, pathways, contemplating logistics, and applying it to their plan.

Lom looked down first at the turquoise sea and its tan-colored sand, then onto a dock lined with fishing boats. Suddenly, he had a flash of inspiration, an epiphany, and the plan unfolded before his eyes. He knew what he had to do to complete this mission successfully.

Mensch instructed his driver to take the men's luggage to their rooms. Once alone in Lom's room, Mensch politely suggested that they turn their energy toward business. Lom slowly reached into the inner pocket of his jacket and held up an envelope for Mensch to see.

"The guns, please," was all Lom said. Mensch nodded and reached into his attaché case and took out two guns–both automatic and both forty caliber. One was a Glock twenty-two like Toby used back in New York; the other was a forty-caliber Smith & Wesson, which used a rimless pistol cartridge. Lom felt more comfortable with the Glock, but since Toby had used it in New York, he figured he'd let him keep that one and he'd take the S&W. The gun didn't matter. He knew he was an excellent shot.

"What about ammo?" Lom asked. Mensch produced two boxes of forty-caliber ammunition, fifty rounds to a box. This was a bit overkill, but Lom loved the security he felt with it in his possession. "The suppressors?" Once again, Mensch reached into his attaché case and, this time, handed Lom two plain narrow boxes.

"These were very difficult to get," Mensch said. "I had to call in a lot of favors, but I managed. So please, check them out. I want to make sure that they satisfy you before I leave." Mensch would only get paid if his customer was satisfied.

"Good," Lom said after opening the boxes and snapping the silencers onto the automatics. Satisfied, he handed Mensch the stuffed envelope. Mensch took a moment to count the money, stood, and extended his hand toward Lom. Lom eyed him and reciprocated, gripping his hand.

"It was a pleasure doing business with you. Here is my card. Should you ever require my services again?" Mensch clicked his heals, gave Lom a slight bow, and left. This was the first time Lom had ever had someone click his heals intentionally at him. He picked up the house phone, called Charlie, then Toby, and asked them to come to his room.

Charlie and Toby arrived moments later. Lom opened the door and peered up and down the hallway. He locked and bolted the hotel room entrance. Lom handed Toby the Glock twenty-two, a silencer, and a box of ammunition. "Damn," Lom said. "I forgot to ask for extra magazines, but too late to worry about it now. We'll have to settle with one."

While Toby was loading his forty-caliber rounds, Charlie got busy trying to secure a small boat, following Lom's orders. He didn't care if he bought it or rented it, but Lom wanted a boat before they left on their mission.

Small talk aside, the three men sat down to rehash logistics and fine tune the plan. Lom looked at Toby. "Toby, maybe it would be better if you went with Charlie to get the boat because you speak the language and it would be less suspicious, but be careful. I don't need you or your voice being recognized. We don't need the whole town out in the streets shouting 'THE KING IS BACK, THE KING IS BACK.' We can't afford to let the cat out of the bag too soon. And make sure the boat you get has ample sleeping quarters below. I don't know how many we'll be taking, so make sure that we have enough room down below so they won't see us from above. I want it to look like just another boat sitting among a lot of other boats. When you get back, we'll go down to the dining room and have us some supper. Then we'll wait. We'll leave the hotel close to midnight and make our way up to the castle. Toby, do you have any way to get us inside the castle with no one knowing?"

Toby smiled and said, "When we get to the castle, leave everything to me."

Chapter Nineteen

The little skiff bumped against the piling of the small dock that was nestled at the base of the castle. The local fishermen used the dock. A man jumped off the boat and splashed into the shallow water. His bare feet settled into the fine white sand, his shoes tied securely around his neck to keep them dry. Lom had learned this lesson the hard way in Korea when he had no choice but to walk in swamps and rivers with his boots on. A severe case of dry rot will do it. Old habits die hard, so Lom kept his boots dry by hanging them around his neck like a large necklace.

Toby whispered to his two friends, "Follow me. Say nothing." He led them up a winding path surrounded by a canopy of thick green. The bushes impeded the view from above onlookers. They walked up hill after hill for approximately twenty minutes until they arrived at the base of the castle's eastern wall. Toby, with Lom and Charlie trailing behind, followed the wall to where the corners met and motioned for them to stop.

"There's a secret entrance that leads into the castle," Toby said. "They originally constructed it into the design of the castle when it was first built back in eighteen fifty-nine. No one knows about it but the first son of the King, who they swore to secrecy. My orders are never to reveal it to anyone, including my brothers, sisters, family members, and especially to anyone outside of the palace. I am breaking my vow by telling you where it is. If I don't return, you now know of it. If I am not back within the hour, you must enter the castle. That means they have captured me and imprisoned me, along with my men. To enter, you must press on this stone with all of your strength." Toby pointed to the cornerstone on the sixth row from the bottom. "Watch what happens when I press this stone. Notice that you will hear the lock release and the wall will open. When that happens, push hard and the wall will swing in. By pushing the stone inward, you release a catch, which allows the wall to swing free of the locking mechanism. Once you enter the castle, walk along the narrow passage until you see two flights of stairs. Take the steps leading down. They lead to the dungeon. You must tread softly or the guards on that post will hear your steps. The guards will not see you because it will hide you behind the dungeon's wall, but they will certainly hear your steps if you are not careful. I'm going in now. Look at the time on your watch and if I'm not back in one hour, then either go back to the boat or come into the castle and get me."

"Don't you worry about me going back to the boat," Lom replied. "'Cause if you're not back in this exact spot in one hour, then by God, I'll be coming in."

Toby pushed the stone so hard that his face turned a crimson color. The secret door groaned and grated a bit as stone moved against stone, revealing a narrow passage. Toby slipped into the darkness. The men watched the stone wall slowly return to its closed position and Lom murmured to Charlie, "Hell, Charlie, and we thought we were the only ones with secret places and stuff. Our place is Mickey Mouse compared to this. This is ROMANCING THE STONE shit. Hmmm," he said. "Must be another tripping mechanism inside the wall that causes it to return and move back into place. Can hardly tell there's a secret entrance and we're looking right at it. Boy, that's some terrific engineering, if I say so myself."

The two men sat down under a tree and waited, mindful of each second. Seconds turned to minutes. They remarked on how long a minute can be when doing nothing. The hour arrived and no Toby. Lom instructed Charlie to stay put for an extra fifteen minutes.

"Okay, Charlie, that's our cue. He should have been here." The two men rose to their feet. "Time to get the boat ready. I'm going in." Lom pressed on the stone and as he did, it opened effortlessly. With a small amount of light illuminating his face, there stood Toby with two women trailing behind him.

"Toby! Boy, am I glad to see you," Lom said, smiling like an old proud papa. "I was just about to go in and get you, my friend."

Toby smiled and said, "Mother, I would like to introduce you to two very dear friends of mine, Charlie and Lom. Gentlemen, my dear mother, Queen Isabella. Also, meet my fiancée, Svetlana."

Lom looked at Charlie, then at the two women. "Well, I sure am proud to meet you ladies, and if I don't say so myself, ma'am, you have raised one manly son and you should be very proud of yourself." Then he took the Queen's hand in his and said, "It is my esteemed pleasure to meet you, Your Majesty," and he kissed her hand ever so slightly.

The Queen responded, "Mr. Lom, the pleasure is mine."

Next, Lom gently clasped Svetlana's hand and remarked, "I will say this about that young rascal. He sure has good taste in women and I am pleased to make your acquaintance, Ms. Svetlana. Now, I would suggest that you ladies go on with Charlie here and he'll see that you get safely to the boat. Toby here and I need to go inside and take care of a little business."

"Agreed," said the Queen. "We need to make haste from the castle grounds. It won't be long before someone will notice our absence."

The women moved quickly and anxiously. Charlie led the way back down the winding path now hidden by the darkness of the moonless night. Heavy indigenous foliage provided a shield. Toby and Lom watched as they vanished into the night.

Lom nudged Toby on the elbow. "Come on. Let's get going."

Toby shook his head and said, "No. You can't come with me, Lom. Wait here. If I don't come out in a half hour, then you come for me."

"Wait a minute, son," Lom answered. "I can't just be wasting my time waiting on you all the time out here and twiddling my thumbs."

"Look, Lom, if we both go in and we both get caught, who's going to rescue us? Don't you get it? This time, I need YOU to watch MY back. The first time I went in, I took the stairs up to the bedrooms. I was lucky to find my mother and my fiancée in the same room and could bring them out without being seen. But now, I'm taking the steps leading down into the dungeon. My head of security, Karl Swensen, is in one of those cells and the rest of my men are in the others. I have to get Karl and my men out. If all goes well, I should be out within a half hour. There are usually no guards down there at this time of night because there's no need for them to be there. The prisoners are all locked up, so why have men guarding them when we could use them elsewhere? If I'm successful, I'll be back."

"Well," Lom moaned. "It makes sense to me. I don't have to like it, but go on. Go get everybody, King. And, hey, don't push it this time. Thirty minutes is thirty minutes, okay?"

Toby nodded in agreement, turned, and re-entered the passageway leading to the castle. Lom counted leaves, doing anything to bide the time. Waiting sure is hard work, he thought, much harder than doing. Lom liked the action and these past few weeks were like a blood transfusion to a dying man. He felt alive again and, with Martha in the picture now, he felt a stirring, this time in his loins. The old man hadn't felt this way in years. Thoughts of this special lady occupied his mind, and before he knew it, a half hour had come and gone. He suddenly snapped out of his reverie and looked at his watch. Forty-five had passed. He was furious with himself.

"Damnit, Martha, look what you did to me. Damnit. Women! Just leave it to women to mess things up even when they're not around," he said out loud. "Toby must be in a lot of trouble. Damn!"

Lom rushed to the special stone built into the wall and pushed it like Toby had instructed. He listened for the click of the mechanism to release and watched in admiration as the hidden door in the wall swung inward. Leaning forward, he pushed it open the rest of the way and began his trek into the narrow passageway, turning around to acknowledge the door as it closed into the stone wall, becoming once again a seamless part of the structure. Lom walked, almost on his toes, mindful of Toby's warning about how the sound of his feet would travel. Soon, he approached the set of stairs, remembering Toby's words. He began his descent down three flights. On each level, he caught glimpses into the castle though gratings spaced every few feet. So far, there was nothing unusual. At the third level, he recognized what seemed to be a dungeon. Careful to stand back away from the cutouts in the wall, he slowly inched his face closer to the tiny peephole. There he was. In the center of the dank, cold room, there was Toby hanging upside down all trussed up like a Thanksgiving turkey, with his hands tied behind his back and his feet bound at the ankles. Toby was turning, slowly, in a precise circular pattern, just like a rotisserie. Lom waited for a moment, mindful of others in the room. He repositioned himself behind the opening, moved side to side, gazing at the room from every angle, as much as the small hole would allow. Lom leaned in, placed his full face and eyes right into the holes, blocking all light. At about his tenth revolution, Toby's eyes locked onto the grating, something he must have been doing anxiously for a while, Lom reckoned. This time, his eyes fixated on the face behind the hole with a look that said, "And where the hell have you been while I've been swinging like a corpse on the gallows?"

Lom moved his lips, hoping Toby could read them as he mouthed the words. "Psst. Yep, it's me," he whispered as he tried to decide what to do next. He didn't have a clue. Lom had always trusted his intuition... and his luck. It had brought him safely home after three tours in Korea. Working slowly, he carefully began carving into the perimeter of the grating, to no avail. It didn't budge. He repeated the carving action until, one by one, each side gave way. With a little muscle, he pried it the rest of the way with his knife. He waited about a minute and pulled the grating aside a few inches, just enough for him to see if anyone else was in the room. He saw no one other than Toby and a bunch of bars; cells, he surmised. There were faint murmurs emanating from the cells. Now was the time. Lom readied himself by placing his right foot down from his hidden position behind the wall. Suddenly, there were footsteps. A uniformed man, dressed in bright colors of red and yellow, entered, followed by two guards in what appeared to be military or royal garb. Lom reached for the grill and whipped it back into position. He listened.

The man in the red and yellow walked toward Toby. "So, how are you enjoying this special place, Toby? The dungeon has a special charm, don't you think?" the man taunted. Toby did not respond. "So, we're not talking right now. Tell me, Toby, can you feel your feet? What's wrong? Your face looks a little red."

Toby replied, "My face is red from anger. But never mind, there are worse things in life. This is nothing more than a minor annoyance," he said. Lom could see that the King was in pain.

Lom reached for his gun and took aim. He felt the impulse to shoot all three of them right there on the spot, but common sense prevailed and he waited, all the while reminding himself that you should never kill someone from emotion. He had learned that in the war. Murder was a part of self-defense and survival, but in other instances, it must be methodical in order to be effective.

"I just came down to see how you were doing, brother, but it looks like you're not in the chatting mood. Sad, so sad, Toby, that it had to come to this," the leader continued. That was all Lom needed. Confirmed. That buzzard was Toby's brother. Lom listened to the brother talk a lot of nonsense, never receiving answers from a bound man. Lom never wanted to kill a man as badly as he did at this moment. But he waited patiently until the man was tired of talking to himself. Toby's brother, receiving no satisfaction from Toby's silence, turned, gave a wave to his men, and exited the dungeon, slamming the door behind them, setting off a loud reverberating clang. Lom waited a few seconds, and once again, pulled the grating aside. One foot at a time, he swung himself over the grid's ledge and made his way down onto the stone floor of the dungeon. He set into action, first loosening Toby's restraints and then using his Randall fighting knife and, working quickly, cut the ropes binding Toby–hands first, then feet. Cradling his arms around the King, he guided his unbound legs onto the ground as Toby braced himself with his hands. The two men fell backwards onto the cold floor.

"Thanks, Lom. What took you so long?" Toby smiled as he stumbled around on the floor.

"Thought I'd make it a little more interesting, King. Nothing like taking it to the edge," Lom replied.

The room erupted in soft words as eyes peering through the iron slats gazed in disbelief.

"Shhh..." Toby cautioned. "Quiet! Not a word until we're out of here. Got that?" The prisoners nodded in agreement.

Toby, still wobbly, stood and walked a few steps at a time as he tried to get his sea legs, waiting impatiently for his blood to flow in the right direction. "Over there. The keys," Toby said. Lom walked to a rack on the wall that held rows of keys.

"Which one, Toby? Hell, there are twenty keys here."

"The one on the bottom right," Toby said. "It's the master key. All the others are spares."

Toby wasted no time. He opened the cell doors, releasing his men one at a time. He started with the cell nearest the entrance and worked his way around the circle until he reached the complete opposite side of the door. The circle was complete. All cells were empty. As Lom was beginning a head count, one man rushed forward, embraced Toby, and knelt before him. "Your Majesty," he said.

"It's good to see you are still alive, Karl. Now get off your knees, please. Right now, protocol doesn't exist. We have to get out of here. "

"It's good to see you too, Your Majesty."

Toby pointed to one man. "Hans, check the door to see if it's locked." Hans bowed and rushed over to the steel door. Even though it had clanged shut after Lars had left, oddly enough, it hadn't locked.

"Okay, men, let's move out," the King ordered. "Follow me, but do so quietly. Remember, these stone walls echo so that they can hear even a mouse tip-toe upstairs."

Lom stood back for a moment, drinking in how this once beaten down, hunted young man had almost instantly converted to a stately aristocrat with a regal presence, a King who commanded respect and whose orders they obeyed without question. Toby was in complete control. As they were about to ascend the stairs, Toby insisted that the old man stay close behind him. Bewilderment set into the faces of the prisoners as many of the men wondered why the King wanted to have an old man behind him and not one of his highly trained military officers.

One level up from the dungeon was the sleeping quarters for the King's guard. Toby peeked around the wall at the top of the stairs. No one was present. In single file, the men walked quietly past the bunkroom to the armory in the rear of the large room. They entered the door to the armory. They traveled a short distance to a cage. Inside, clearly visible, were weapons of every kind — all sizes, shapes, and models of guns. Toby tugged on the cage. They locked it.

"Step aside, Toby," Lom ordered. The moment Toby's body cleared the cage, Lom fired, and the little gun flashed as it spit a silenced shot, bull's eye, right into the lock, causing it to fly off the hasp. The men rushed the cage, helping themselves to small arms and semi-automatic machine guns. Methodically, they passed out ammo, ensuring that each man had what he needed. All weapons in Talvania used forty-caliber bullets, even the machine guns. That made it easy. Lom smirked, reached into a box, and pulled out a few hand grenades, which he stuffed into his pocket. The men checked and rechecked their weapons, ensuring that their guns were fully loaded. Satisfied, Toby motioned for them to move forward, Toby leading the way, with Lom following closely behind. They walked up several sets of stairs until they reached the main level.

Lars had stationed a skeletal crew of guards on duty now that they confined his brother and his men. The newly released men moved steadily forward toward the guards. They listened as the guards, exuberant and proud of their dungeon prize, bragged about the enormous coup — capturing a king and securing the throne for their new boss — something that just didn't happen every day. The guards laughed and joked about how secure their jobs were now. It was the boisterous sound of revelry, a cause for celebration. The men passed around a jug, each taking turns, one swig at a time, singing all the while. Slurred words and the slight weaving of bodies showed their faculties were likely impaired.

It was only when he discovered that his mother and Svetlana were missing that he knew it was Toby's doing. Toby's next move was simple. He would return to free his faithful followers. Lars had alerted his off duty men to report back to work. No one was to be granted time off; They warned all guards to remain vigilant. The false King threatened the men with their lives and those of their loved ones if they made mistakes. He clarified that King Torbjorn was somewhere very near, and he ordered his men to do nothing if they saw him enter the castle.

It had worked. When Toby slipped into the castle through a secret door in the dungeon's corner, he did not know of Lars cleverly hatched plan. Lars men waited until Toby had entered the basement room and, like a swarm of bees, descended on him in droves. Toby had been out planned and out manned. Toby's men were the cheese, and the dungeon was the mousetrap. Lars had even gone a step further. Knowing that his brother could do nothing without his men, he had cleverly planted a dozen of his own men in the cells.

Now that he had captured his brother, Lars planned to use some torture, but nothing too severe. When he felt his brother was at his breaking point, he would lock him into one of the dungeon cells and keep him there forever. As much as greed and power consumed him, Lars still did not want his mother harmed any more emotionally than necessary. For years, he had held the secret ambition to take over the throne. When his brother confided in him he was speaking before the U.N., Lars knew that this was his chance. He set about finding the best men in America for the job, carefully asking a small group of insiders who they would entrust with a secret mission that might involve assassination. Lars had implied that the job was to prevent civil unrest in his country. It had taken months to find the right candidates. Becker was the man.

Lars welcomed Becker to Talvania to discuss the contract. He needed to see the headman in person, look into his eyes, and find out whether he possessed the smarts and the beastly instincts needed to ensure success. Becker was fierce. Money talked. Lars knew Becker would instruct his men to kill the King if it became a necessity, but he reconciled this by convincing himself that he never gave an order to Becker to kill his brother. He had assigned his trusted men to meet with Becker for the more serious discussion and negotiation; therefore, his conscience was clear, he reminded himself.

Lars had watched Becker from a monitor in another room, observing his eyes, his handshake, his body language as he first met with Lars' military personnel. Lars would have plausible deniability. There was only one American involved in the contract talks with Becker, and that was Kurt, the leader of the gang. The American had hesitated before accepting the contract. Killing a king would bring an almost insurmountable amount of pressure on him and his organization. He risked losing money from other operations, as he would have to lie low, hide out, if the facts ever showed that Kurt and his gang murdered the King of Talvania. Becker had sealed the deal by offering the American two million dollars up front and another two million when the job was complete. Kurt had argued for the four million up front, but Becker stood firm. He was no business fool. Paying up front was little incentive to carry out a contract. The King would die in order to prevent unrest and Lars, as next in line, would ascend the throne and make sweeping changes that would positively affect every Talvanian household.

Now that he had imprisoned Toby, the saga was complete. He would remain there until his death, eating and sleeping among a host of other men loyal to Toby, and others who had committed other offences such as blue-collar crime or those who had the audacity to line up against Lars' political views.

Toby and his men rushed into the throne room on both sides. Lars men, due to drink, were a little slow to react. Lom took aim and shot the first man, who reached for his gun. A second man went for his weapon and ducked behind a table. Lom timed his shot perfectly. Bam–right in the head as the man was lining up a shot at Toby. Two other half-dazed men, with guns drawn, attempted to rush the King from behind. They were too slow for Lom, who, through instinctive anticipation, fired at both before either could get off a shot. Toby's men's eyes were broad, hardly believing what this old man had just done. Lom popped off four more shots, leveling all four before any of Toby's men could respond. The sharp-shooting exhibition was over.

They quickly rounded leftovers of Lars men up before they could mount a counter-offensive. The men were well aware of the futility of fighting any longer. It was a lose-lose proposition. They threw down their weapons, signaling surrender. Toby and Lom pointed their weapons at them and motioned toward the wall. The men lined up, facing the wall with their hands held high above their heads. At that moment, Lars entered the room. Looking confused, he first glanced at his men and then at Toby. Toby called out to Lom, "Cover me," and aimed his gun toward his brother.

"Toby," Lom said, "It's going to be all right." Lars tried to wrap his head around what was happening. His plan had worked perfectly. He had captured his brother and his right to the throne was assured. What went wrong? How could this have happened? How could everything right go so wrong so fast?

Lom walked over to Lars, put his face to his, and glared, positioning his gun underneath his chin. "If you weren't Toby's brother, I would kill you right now, right where you're standing without so much as a New York minute of thought. In fact, I think I'll kill you anyway." Lom moved his gun from his chin and buried it deep into Lars' shoulder. Before Toby could speak, he pulled the trigger. Lars face grimaced in pain. He grasped his shoulder and slumped to the floor.

"No. Lom, don't shoot him again. No."

"Hell, Toby," Lom said smiling. "I just gave him a little boo-boo like a little bee sting. He needs to feel a little pain. It's nothing compared to the pain he's caused you."

Lom raised his gun, put it against Lars other shoulder, and taunted, "How about we even it out a bit? One bullet on each side should do it. Nice and level. I like things that are even. I'm kinda anal about that."

Lars whimpered, "Please, no. Toby, don't let him. Please."

Toby gingerly tugged on Lom's arm, drawing him back, and put out his hand. "Give me the gun, Lom."

Lom hesitated a moment, then he turned his gun, butt end, and with that lopsided smile of his, said, "I was just funning with you, Toby. I wasn't gonna plug him again. But I got a little pleasure seeing that scared look on his ugly face. Come on, Toby, admit that scared look was worth all the trouble you went through."

"Okay, here... it's yours." Toby stared at the weapon for a long moment, drinking in what had happened. He took the gun and placed it on the table along with the other weapons the King's men had taken from Lars loyals.

"You won't need it anymore, Lom," Toby said. "It's over. Besides, you can't take it with you when you leave the country, so it's just as well I take it from you now."

"Whatever you say, partner, uh, Your Majesty. No, I don't think I can say that. I'll have to stick with Toby, if you don't mind."

Chuckling a bit, Toby replied, "No, Lom, I really don't mind." The King's words rang with affection. Lom gave Toby a mischievous smile and countered, "Well, since you took my gun, I suppose you want these li'l ole hand grenades too."

Lom walked down to the pier to collect the ladies. Charlie was standing guard and sprang up from the boat as Lom approached. The Queen looked up at Lom and asked, "Where's Toby?"

"Toby's fine, Queen."

"What about Lars? Is he hurt?"

"Well, Lars suffered a minor casualty, but he'll be all right. He had to be taught a lesson. I don't know what Toby's gonna do with him, but that one is a completely different boy from Toby. Toby is a kind and decent fella–not a nasty bone in his body and he has courage like you wouldn't believe. I'm sorry to say this because he's your son, and I don't really mean to hurt you, but Lars should have been killed, or at the very least put in the same dungeon where he put Toby, and if I had any say in the matter, I'd throw away the key. I'm really sorry, ma'am, to have to tell you this, and I sure don't mean any disrespect."

The Queen, with all the stoicism she could muster, replied, "Thank you. Thank you, Mr. Lom, for that news," as she battled a tiny tear, determined to win. The tear got the best of her and trickled from the corner of her right eye, leaving a trail of light as it washed away some of her regally applied make-up. And as quickly as the tear had appeared, the Queen, with a faint smile, looked at Lom and said, "There's no disrespect taken, Mr. Lom. Torbjorn told me, in the brief time we had together, what you did for him. You have a mother's deepest thank you for protecting her son."

Lom blushed and replied, "Shucks, ma'am, it was nothing. I came to love that boy. He's special."

At that moment, Toby came strolling up. "Lom, I knew I'd find you here. Come with me for a moment. I want to give you something."

"Come on, Charlie," Lom said as he grabbed the hand of each woman and placed their arms interlocking his. Flanked by one woman on the right, another on the left, side by side, they strolled by the winding paths as he regaled the women with war stories all the way back to the castle. Laughter filled the air. As they entered the opulent royal home, Toby said, "Excuse me, everyone, but Lom and I have to talk for a moment." He motioned toward a corridor.

Lom followed Toby into a sitting room, close to the throne room, that had a little table, probably for sipping tea or something. Together they sat, just the two of them, quiet for a few seconds. Toby then reached into his pocket and removed a small box. "Here, Lom. This is for you. I want you to take it back to America. You go find Martha and give this to her. She's a fine woman, and she loves you."

"What is this, Toby?"

"Open it."

Lom slowly lifted the cover off of the little box.

"Toby, I can't take this. Are you crazy, boy? This is just, well, it's just too much."

"Take it, Lom. You're in my country now. It's an order from your king. Give it to Martha."

"Wait a minute now, young fella. An order from MY king? I don't have a king."

"You do now. You are now an honorary citizen of Talvania, so... if you don't obey me, I can legally place you into one of those nice, dark, cold cells in the dungeon." He chuckled.

"Ha! Okay. Okay. Enough. You convinced me." Lom laughed.

"But, Lom," Toby said. "It comes with a condition. You may give it to her in the States, but," he paused, "you must bring her here to get married. Surprise her. Take her on a special trip. Then you'll come here, where the citizens of Talvania and I will give her the wedding beyond all weddings. You must give me your word that you'll abide by what the King has said."

Lom, a little overwhelmed, seemed to drift for a moment. "Okay, King," he said. "But I'd like to have a little condition on my end, too, a little extra favor, if I'm not being ungrateful."

"What is that?" Toby asked, unsure of what to expect.

"I'd like to bring Charlie with me if it's all right with you."

Toby laughed out loud. The first time Lom had really ever heard him let loose like that. "Forget about that," he said. "I already invited him. He'll be your best man and I'll, if I'm not being too presumptuous, I will give away the bride."

"Wow," Lom replied. "I'm impressed, sonny. You work fast now, don't ya? How in the hell did you plan all of that in the one hour since we stormed the castle? You're gonna make one heck of a king. I can tell you that."

Toby arranged flights for Lom and Charlie back to the States. It was now up to Lom to obey the King's orders. When they completed their plans and he and Martha were ready to come to Talvania, Lom was to give the King a few days' notice. Someone would then escort them back to the country in style.

Chapter Twenty

Wednesday evening, at exactly seven p.m., Lom walked into the Good Burger on Second Avenue. He walked, unnoticed, to his favorite booth. It was taken, so he took the only empty booth he could find, the last booth at the far end, the one farthest from the door. It wasn't long before he saw Martha back out of the kitchen through the swinging doors, balancing a large tray of food. Amazing how she could do that and still have all that food make it to the table each time, he thought. As long as he could remember, he had never seen her drop a tray, not once in the seven years that he had frequented this place. Martha whipped around and headed for her tables, but glanced toward the back of the room and stopped dead in her tracks. A big smile consumed her face. Hastily, she set down the food and rushed over to Lom's table, but as she approached, she restrained herself, plopped down across from him, and asked, "Is it over?"

"Well," Lom smiled, "that depends on what you mean by 'Is it over?'"

"Okay, now, you old geezer. Don't play games with me. 'Is it over' means 'is it over'?"

"Well, yes, and no. One part is over, but another is just beginning, I think. I mean, I hope. Ah, hell, Martha. Now there's nothing left for me to do but..." and his voice trailed off.

Lom slowly reached into his inside jacket pocket and pulled out the little box that Toby had given him and placed it into the center of the coffee shop table where it sat for a moment.

Martha's eyes, fixated, watched as Lom gently nudged the little package across the table toward her.

"Lom, what is this?" she asked. "Are you trying to make up for all the grief you've given me over all these years?"

"Go ahead. Open it," he said. She picked up the little box, held it for a moment, and removed the top. She gasped. "My God, this ring is beautiful. I've seen nothing like it in my life."

"Marry me, Martha. I mean, will you marry me, Martha? I know I'm older and I know I get into a bit of trouble sometimes, but..."

"Oh shut up, you ole worrier," she said as tears rolled down her cheeks. She jumped up from her seat and, as Lom stood up, she wrapped her arms around him, squeezing him tightly and holding herself close to him for what seemed to be an eternity.

"Well, is that a yes? I mean, is it you like the ring or are you getting what I'm saying?"

"Yes," Martha replied, fighting back the tears. "Yes, Lom. I've loved you for years. Yes, yes. Oh, Lom, I can't believe this. YES."

"Martha, you are just about to quit this job. I'm going to take good care of you for the rest of your life. Now, you just decide when you can kiss this place goodbye and let me know, 'cause you and I will take a brief trip. Remember when I promised you that if I made it back, you and I would take a trip? Well, pack your bags. It's time."

"Yes, I remember. Let's see... I can have Rosalie cover for me while I'm gone. I'm sure she could use the extra money. Well... give me a few days to arrange things. Then I'll be free to go with you on that trip. Can I ask you where we'll be going?"

"Martha, Rosalie will not cover for you while you're gone. Rosalie may need some help. You don't have to work anymore. And no, I can't tell you where we're going–it's a surprise, but... I can tell you this. You'll never forget it."

Monday afternoon, Lom called Kurt. He answered, and bracing for bad news, was silent for a moment.

"Sorry, Kurt, that things didn't go as I planned, so I'm just gonna have to come over there and kill you," Lom said.

"Why? What happened?" Kurt barked. "I knew it. Things are never that easy. Never. Now what? We're back to square one."

"Ah, Kurt, ye of little faith. How are you doing?"

"Well, I would be better if you'd had good news, but now, well, not so great."

"Kurt, I'm just messing with you. No worries at all. They paid your debt in full. You don't have a thing to worry about from here on out unless you forget the promise you made and try to hurt me or mine. Why then, I'd have no choice but to find you and then we're talking some great bodily harm. But that aside, everything is fine. I just wanted to call you and let you know I kept my promise and fixed things right proper."

Kurt let out an audible sigh that Lom heard clearly through the phone. "Good. I'm glad it's over. And I don't have to worry about any more of my men being killed by an old man? How I can ever explain that to the rest of my men is beyond me. But now that this nastiness is all behind us, I would like to know your name."

"Why?"

"Because I need to know the name of the man who almost killed me."

"Well, I don't really see what difference it makes, but okay, my friends call me Lom. Satisfied?"

"One more thing before we end our conversation. Well, make that two more things. First, I'd like to call you Lom, if that's all right with you?"

"Sure, partner. That's fine with me."

"You are one piece of work, Lom," he affectionately added. Kurt had read somewhere that the Indians used to measure their greatness by the greatness of their enemies. Kurt felt that way about Lom. He was the only man he could think of whose friendship might matter. He respected him that much. Kurt said, "I'd like to meet you in person now that it's over like we talked about before." Lom, even though he was still a little suspicious, thought for a moment, and agreed. He recalled giving Kurt his word on this.

"How about tomorrow morning at the pawnshop?" Lom asked.

"Sounds great. What time is good for you?" Kurt countered.

"I don't know. How's ten tomorrow morning sound?"

"Sounds great," Kurt agreed. "I'll see you at ten, then."

Lom had to admit he was a little curious about Kurt. The man sounded sincere and all, and Lom was a pretty good reader of people. That was one of his talents that had kept him alive all these years. Lom would go with his hunch and meet the man, the same man who had been trying to kill him.

At ten a.m. the next morning, a black Mercedes pulled up to the front of the pawnshop. Three men stepped out of the car and walked through the front door. The little bell on the door tinkled, alerting those inside that someone had entered. Lom sat nonchalantly in a chair with his feet up on Charlie's desk, a bored look on his face and his old nineteen eleven Colt forty-five automatic resting on his lap. Charlie was in the corner, holding a shotgun he had just taken in pawn. As Kurt approached, Lom flashed that funny little grin of his and raised the gun in his right hand, his feet still on the desk.

"Am I gonna be needing this little ole gun?"

Kurt opened his coat, each hand holding open one side, and nodded to his men to do the same.

"We didn't come armed," Kurt said. "So, you're the old man that none of my men could kill?" He shook his head and smiled wanly. "I just wanted to meet you face-to-face and, well, no, you don't need that gun. Not today and not any day from now on where it concerns me. My part in this is over. You took me right out of the equation when you took out that phony king. Yeah, I heard all about it. It's all over the news. I learned my lesson, though. I make a good living doing what I do without taking on contracts like this. The money, that irresistible seductress, got to me, you see. I just couldn't turn down that kind of money. I didn't feel right from the beginning, but like I said, I couldn't refuse it, not with the money that guy was paying me." Kurt was comfortable talking about it. The words were spilling out of him now and it was as if he were in the confessional, purging himself of his sins and all the bad that he had caused.

"It won't happen again. You have my word on that," he said. As Kurt was putting on his coat to leave, he looked back at Lom. "You know, you gave me a fright there for a little while, old man."

"Lom. My friends call me Lom," Lom interrupted.

Kurt nodded at the unexpected compliment. He walked over to Lom and extended his hand. Lom looked at his hand for a moment. The men exchanged a firm but cordial handshake, their hands clasped tightly together, just staring into each other's eyes, not saying a word. It was Kurt who broke the silence.

"You know, I never really had a friend before. I have a lot of acquaintances, but not one person I could ever call my friend. Even when we were out to kill each other, I grew to respect you, and I wished I could have stopped what the paid me to do, but the momentum carried all of us in that one direction–the death of you two, and I didn't see any way out of it until you came up with the answer. I was happy and relieved about that. I was looking forward to this meeting so I could tell you this in person. Look, Lom, I'm not good at this sort of thing, but I'd like to make it all up to you, so if I can ever be of service to you, just call me and I'll be there."

Kurt turned and tilted his head in the door's direction. His two men walked ahead of him as usual, checked the street in both directions. The black limousine drove away.

Lom turned to Charlie, who was busy putting the shotgun back into its box. "You know, Charlie, that Kurt fella ain't the worse guy I ever met. I could get to like him if I spent enough time with him. What do you think?"

"I think you taught that man a lesson," Charlie said. "I think he respects you. You humbled him and it looks like no one's ever been able to do that before. Instead of him being pissed off because you killed so many of his men, it came right down to respect. Huh. Respect. That's a big word that packed a powerful punch with him. Mighty strange, but that's what I got out of this meeting."

"So you think that he just wanted to come here to meet the man he grew to respect?"

"Yep. Did you see his eyes light up when you corrected him when he called you 'old man'? You told him 'my friends call me Lom.' It was like you touched a nerve. He even told you to call him if you ever needed him for anything. Now that's some turnaround, if you ask me."

"Yeah, I guess you're right, Charlie. My gut told me everything would work out at today's meeting. I had to look into his eyes for the truth, and that's why I agreed to meet him. He's gonna be a better man because of all this, Charlie. Well, I gotta see Martha now. I'll be back in a couple of hours and tell you all about what happened."

Epilogue

Martha couldn't believe it. They bypassed all the commercial lines at the airport and went straight to a private jet parked on the tarmac. They walked up the short flight of steps leading into the interior of the G5 jet aircraft. Martha stepped into the plane and stopped, overwhelmed by its opulence. She gasped. "Is all this only for us?"

Lom smiled. "Of course it is. When I take a lady on a vacation, I mean to make an impression." Martha laughed and hit him lightly on his arm.

"You sure do!" she said.

The jet glided smoothly along the runway. When it had gained enough forward momentum, it lifted gracefully off the ground, its nose pointed skyward straight into the azure sky before settling onto its designated flight path. Martha settled back into the comfortable recliner and looked out her window, all the while sipping on the champagne that the Talvanian flight attendants had offered. Unaware of who they were, she decided not to ask too many questions. All she knew was that the plane was fancy, the girls were nice, and she felt special.

After cruising for approximately two hours, Martha, Lom, and they gave Charlie menus that featured a host of specialty items. Each opted for a plain old steak. The flight was smooth and relaxing. The three bantered, told jokes, and even napped a bit in between.

Upon arrival, a uniformed officer was waiting by the customs counter. As the three Americans approached, the officer flashed his ID to the man behind the cage, telling him that under special orders of the King, he would take charge and escort them through the airport. The man introduced himself as Henri Kruger, an official aide charged with assisting them with customs and their journey to their hotel.

Martha, who wasn't used to traveling, seemed worried about this man asking for and taking her passport. Lom assured her that the officer was fine. The officer walked slightly ahead of them, bypassing customs. The man named Kruger led them into a small, private room, where he personally stamped their documents and walked them toward the baggage area.

At baggage claim, a man holding a sign that read "Mr. Lom" made his way toward the three visitors. Kruger nodded to him. He instructed another man to collect their suitcases and take them to the car. They parked the official black stretch limousine outside the terminal, in an area marked "Reserved."

It impressed Martha with the cleanliness of Talvania. She asked many questions on the ride to the hotel. People receiving monetary help from the government had to work in some capacity and keep the streets and sidewalks clean. There were no cigarette butts, no gum wrappers anywhere in sight. The buildings were spotless, as if they were just pressure cleaned or repainted. As they drove through the city and into the countryside, Talvania's beauty transfixed Martha. In the distance, she could see an opulent structure. It reminded her of Cinderella's castle at Disney World. What a gorgeous building, she thought. The limousine made its way closer and closer to the building. Martha was perplexed.

A guard peered inside and motioned the car forward after the limousine had arrived at the gate. The drive was about a mile long, a straight shot that led to a large circular driveway. The car came to a halt. Outside stood a young man dressed in a military red and yellow uniform, waiting to greet them. Martha turned to Lom and, just as she was about to ask him something, the door opened and the uniformed man extended his hand, offering her help as she exited the car.

"Lom, how great to see you again, my friend," Toby said.

"You, too, Toby. You too." Toby was the name of the man that Lom had been helping, Martha thought. Toby?

"Martha, I presume?" Toby asked.

"Yes, I'm Martha. So nice to meet you." She barely put two words together. "Toby?" Martha asked.

"Yes, Ms. Martha. It is a pleasure. I look forward to getting to know you. But if you don't mind, I will need you to join your dresser," Toby said.

"Dresser?" Martha asked. "What's a dress?.."

At that moment, a female attendant motioned for Martha to follow her. Off they went through the mirror-lined corridors, past gold-laced ceilings, and into a room that was the most beautiful room Martha had ever seen. A cream-colored canopy with ribbons of blue and purple intertwined, draped over the king-sized bed. Pillows of every size and shape adorned the bed. And the bathroom–the bathroom was complete with a sauna, a steam room, a Jacuzzi, and a tub that could have passed for a swimming pool back home. It was the size of the burger joint! This was almost too much to take in. They placed a variety of flowers in different colors everywhere, coating the room with a symphony of color and filling the air with sweet fragrances.

But it was the dressing room that almost stopped her heart. The attendant opened the large doors. A multitude of beautiful dresses and gowns draped on velvet hangers hung on a rail in the dressing room corner. The attendant took one dress, held it up in front of Martha, and pressed it to her body. She turned Martha slowly toward the mirror, never saying a word. The attendant then took her by her hand and led her to the other end of the dressing room, where a beautiful white wedding dress hung in splendor. Martha looked at it, admiring its detail and elegance. The attendant smiled and removed the gown from its hanger and asked her to try it on. Martha was confused, but she did as she was told. Martha slipped into the dress and whirled around like a schoolgirl. This was fun. The attendant busied herself with pins and tucked in seams, working every inch of the dress from top to bottom.

"All done," the attendant said. "Thank you for your patience."

"This dress is magnificent. Can I ask you who it's for?"

The woman answered, "Why it's for you, Madam. That's why I was measuring it. It's for your wedding on Sunday."

"What? I'm getting married on Sunday. This Sunday? This coming Sunday?"

"Yes, Madam, this Sunday and the King himself will give you away. This is a great honor. You must be very special for the King himself to do that."

Martha was speechless. That sly old fox. She looked down at the ring on her finger and back at the beautiful dress. Tears streamed down her face. Martha began getting dressed again.

"No, Madam, put these clothes on instead," the attendant said. And once again, she took Martha by the hand, this time to another dressing room filled with new clothes, the tags still on, minus the price.

"Please try these," the attendant said. "We made them to your measurements and I would like to see how they fit." Martha studied the items. She felt the fabric. These were expensive clothes. She removed a dress from its hanger and was about to put it on, but the woman insisted on helping her. "Wait here," the attendant said as she left. When she reappeared, she was holding a gorgeous pair of shoes and a beautiful hat with matching gloves.

"Good," she said, satisfied with what she saw. "Now, I suggest you slip into something here that's comfortable and please wait here at the mirror." The woman pressed a button and another woman soon joined them.

"This is Sophia," she said. "She will help you with your hair, your nails, and your makeup. My name is Laura. Now I will leave you for a few moments while Sophia works with you. You are quite fortunate, because they know Sophia throughout all of Talvania as the best beautician. I will return when Sophia finished. Then we have one last item of business."

Laura exited, leaving Sophia to work on Martha's hair. She trimmed, colored, and experimented with style after style until she finally uttered, "Voila! That's it." Next, there was the manicure and foot massage.

"I'm not equipped to give you a pedicure," she said apologetically. "But we remedy that during the week when you come to my shop." Sophia, her job complete, pressed a button on the wall at the side of the mirror. Laura opened the door and marched back in.

"Let me look at you. Very good, Sophia. Her fiancé will be pleased. Come, Martha. Let's get you dressed."

Martha dressed as instructed and turned to sneak a peek in the mirror. "Oh, my goodness!" she exclaimed. She felt beautiful. As Martha turned to leave the mirror, Laura said, "Not yet Madam–the finishing touches."

Martha couldn't figure out what the finishing touches could be. She looked at herself in the mirror once again. Her ensemble was complete, right down to the hat and gloves.

"I don't understand," Martha said. "What finishing touches could you possibly be talking about? I have everything. I mean, I have so much of everything that what on earth could be missing?"

"These finishing touches, Madam," she said as she handed Martha a set of diamond earrings and a matching diamond necklace. The necklace had layer after layer of diamonds draped into a V-shaped pattern. They were exquisite! Laura placed the necklace around Martha's neck. Martha giggled with joy. How could a little getaway turn into this? She thought.

Laura interrupted her thoughts, asking, "Are you ready, madam?"

"Yes. I'm ready, but for what, I don't know."

"Let's go downstairs and join the gentlemen."

When Martha walked into the room, Lom was speechless for a moment. "Damn, Martha, but you look beautiful,"

"Lom, I can't believe this," Martha said. Toby walked over to her, glanced at her admiringly, took her gloved hands into his, and looked her up and down. "You look beautiful, but there is still something missing."

"Toby, what more can there possibly be?"

"Well, you haven't met my newly appointed ambassador to America. And you haven't met my personal assistant that will handle all of my affairs in Talvania, have you?"

Martha was confused. "Well, no, I haven't. I mean, I'd love to, but I don't understand what you mean. I mean, why would they want to meet me? I mean, that's politics, right?"

"Well, let's bring them in and see. Maybe you will understand the significance of it all."

The King nodded to the man standing at attention at the door. The man slowly opened the heavy structure, revealing Martha's son and daughter, their faces beaming with smiles, ear to ear.

"Martha, I'd like you to meet my new ambassador to the United States, Thomas Duggan." Tom's face shone like a thousand stars. Martha broke into sobs. Sophia stood at the ready, make-up kit in hand, for any necessary touch-ups.

"And since I don't have a private physician, I want you to meet my new personal doctor, Doctor Daniel Foster. His beautiful wife, Olivia, has agreed to stay and manage my office."

Martha could hardly breathe. Her legs just wouldn't move. She was in shock. Her children ran into their mother's arms and they hugged each other with every ounce of squeeze they could muster. She looked at Toby and mouthed the words "thank you."

Toby, Charlie, and Lom stood quietly–watching, admiring, and soaking up the love that filled the room. It was the moment of all moments. It had all been worth it.

"And now, if you'll please join me," Toby said. "The Queen and Svetlana anxiously await you in the throne room." There was one last order of business by the King regarding a little known American businessman named Victor Franken. They had given him a lucrative five-year contract to import oil into the United States. The King's signature was required and Victor would join the group for the evening.

The following Sunday, Lom and Martha were married in the royal cathedral inside the castle. Charlie was the best man, and Torbjorn Vorland, the King of Talvania, proudly walked the bride down the aisle. The king declared a national holiday. They deemed it LomMart Day in honor of the special couple. It would forever go down in history as a mandated non-work day to symbolize the power of true friendship. Fellow countrymen lined the streets as bands marched and serenaded the newlyweds. The small country celebrated the wedding right alongside the royal family. And since Lom was now an honorary citizen of Talvania, his Royal Highness the King issued a decree commanding him to return once a month to Talvania to act in his official capacity as the King's Royal Premier Fire Arms Coordinator.

Meanwhile, back in America, a man sat in a comfortable leather recliner in front of an enormous television screen, watching a wedding as it streamed live from Talvania. He watched with interest as the wedding of his friend Lom took place in real time. The man smiled; a lit cigar in one hand and a drink in the other. Kurt lifted his glass and said with affection, "This toast is for you, old man."

Thank you for reading my book. I hope you enjoyed reading it as much as I enjoyed writing it. If you liked this story, please leave a review on Amazon.

Joe Corso

Also by Joe Corso

The Comeback
The Time Portal
Lafitte's Treasure
Gunfight in Abilene
Shootout in Cheyenne
The Last Gun-Shark
the Lone Jack Kid series
The Revenge of John W
The Time Traveler series
The Starlight Club series
The Old Man and the King
Engine 24 Fire Stories series
Tommy Topper and the Pixie Princess

www.corsobooks.com

www.ingramcontent.com/pod-product-compliance
Lightning Source LLC
Chambersburg PA
CBHW021015180626
46814CB00003B/1299